'As long as ... bargain.'

Natasha continued, 'This trip ...
business. I'm here to paint and you're here to
drive and protect me from crocodiles. Over
dinner we stick to talking about our trip. Or the
weather. Anything but—' Even to say the
words was likely to inflame the situation.

But Tom said them anyway. 'Anything but us.'
He looked down at her. 'So it's not so much
hate...but fear,' he murmured.

'Fear? You think I'm afraid of you? You must
be mad!'

'Maybe not afraid of me...no,' he conceded.
'More...afraid that you might still have some
feelings. Feelings you don't want to have.'

'Feelings? For you?' She turned on him then.
'I'll tell you what I feel. Nothing. Understand?
Any feelings I had for you, Tom, died long
ago.' Her chest heaved, her breath coming in
furious gulps.

She moaned inwardly. Why was she getting so
steamed up if she felt nothing?

Elizabeth Duke was born in Adelaide, South Australia, but has lived in Melbourne all her married life. She trained as a librarian and has worked in many different types of libraries, but she was always secretly writing. Her first published book was a children's novel, after which she successfully tried her hand at romance writing. She has since given up her work as a librarian to write romance full-time. When she isn't writing or reading, she loves to travel with her husband John, either within Australia or overseas, gathering inspiration and background material for future romances. She and John have a married son and daughter, who now have children of their own.

Recent titles by the same author:

THE PARENT TEST

THE OUTBACK AFFAIR

BY

ELIZABETH DUKE

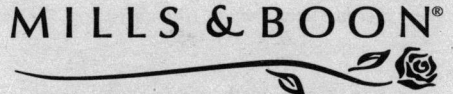

MILLS & BOON®

For Heather and Jan, two talented artists who have
painted, camped and fished at Kakadu. With many thanks.

DID YOU PURCHASE THIS BOOK WITHOUT A COVER?

If you did, you should be aware it is **stolen property** as it was reported
unsold and destroyed by a retailer. Neither the author nor the publisher
has received any payment for this book.

*All the characters in this book have no existence outside the imagination
of the author, and have no relation whatsoever to anyone bearing the
same name or names. They are not even distantly inspired by any
individual known or unknown to the author, and all the incidents are
pure invention.*

*All Rights Reserved including the right of reproduction in whole or in
part in any form. This edition is published by arrangement with
Harlequin Enterprises II B.V. The text of this publication or any part
thereof may not be reproduced or transmitted in any form or by any
means, electronic or mechanical, including photocopying, recording,
storage in an information retrieval system, or otherwise, without the
written permission of the publisher.*

*This book is sold subject to the condition that it shall not, by way of
trade or otherwise, be lent, resold, hired out or otherwise circulated
without the prior consent of the publisher in any form of binding or
cover other than that in which it is published and without a similar
condition including this condition being imposed on the subsequent
purchaser.*

*MILLS & BOON and MILLS & BOON with the Rose Device
are registered trademarks of the publisher.*

*First published in Great Britain 2000
Harlequin Mills & Boon Limited,
Eton House, 18-24 Paradise Road, Richmond, Surrey TW9 1SR*

© Elizabeth Duke 2000

ISBN 0 263 82062 9

*Set in Times Roman 10½ on 12½ pt.
02-0003-40509*

*Printed and bound in Spain
by Litografia Rosés, S.A., Barcelona*

CHAPTER ONE

NATASHA was putting the finishing touches to her oil painting of Ayers Rock when her father poked his head round the door of her studio. 'There's someone to see you, Nat.'

Something in his tone brought her head up sharply. 'Who is it?'

'It's Tom Scanlon.'

She dropped her paintbrush. Heat rushed to her face, then receded, leaving an icy, numbing coldness. She felt as if her lifeblood were draining out of her. It was eighteen months since she'd last seen or heard of her ex-fiancé, and she'd thought he was out of her life for good.

With an effort she unlocked her parched lips. 'Send him away. I don't want to see him.'

'But he's—'

'Tell him I'm busy. I can't come.' How dare Tom Scanlon come back into her life, after what he did to her? How dare he show up here, without warning, and expect her to welcome him with open arms? 'Better still, tell him I don't *want* to see him. Now or ever.'

'If you don't come, Nat, he's likely to barge in here himself. He seems very determined to see you.'

'And I'm just as determined not to see him.'

But underneath her cold resolve her stomach was churning; her nerves fraying. Why had Tom Scanlon come back to visit her after the callous way he'd walked out on her, just two weeks after he'd proposed marriage and sworn undying love? Why was he so determined to see her? To find out if she'd managed to survive without him?

'If you don't speak to him now, love, you'll be looking over your shoulder every time you go out. If you don't want to see him again, Nat, *you* tell him.'

She sighed, clenching her teeth. 'Right. I'll do that. Send him in, Charlie. I'll give him one minute.' Since she and her father had become business partners a year ago—together they owned an art gallery and framing business—she'd fallen into the habit of calling him 'Charlie' rather than 'Dad.' She trembled to think what she would have done without her father in the past year and a half. He'd kept her busy, kept her spirits up, given her a reason for going on...and not looking back.

And now here he was, calmly thrusting Tom Scanlon back into her life!

'Give him a chance, Nat,' Charlie appealed to her. 'At least listen to him. He seems a changed man. There's something...' At her glowering glance, he shrugged. 'Okay, okay, I'll send him in.' He swung on his heel.

But before he reached the door, a tall figure filled the doorway.

'Hullo, Natasha.'

The room tilted. She blinked, her heart turning over. She had to grip her easel for support.

He looked so different from the way he'd looked eighteen months ago. He'd always been a large man, tall and massive shouldered, with a solid, powerful build—perhaps verging on overweight back then. Now he looked—she swallowed—he looked fantastic…leaner, fitter, and healthier than she'd ever seen him before. He must be thirty-six by now, but he looked younger.

Had his new girlfriend done that for him?

Her eyes turned to silver ice. It was a mistake, agreeing to see him—even if only to order him out of her life. It was stirring up all kind of sensations— sensations she'd thought buried for all time.

Her father was edging away. 'I'll leave you two to—'

'No need to go, Dad!' Her voice was sharp, and unnaturally high. The betraying 'Dad' had slipped out. 'Mr. Scanlon won't be staying.'

Her eyes raked coldly over her unwanted visitor. She narrowed her gaze, a tremor quivering through her.

This wasn't the Tom Scanlon she'd known and fallen in love with. This was a stranger—a clean-shaven stranger with a brand-new look, a brand-new

vitality. Where was the ruffianly beard and the un-
tamed mane of long brown hair that had curled over
his collar and tumbled over his brow? Where were
the washed-out jeans and the bush shirt with the
rolled-up sleeves? Where were the dusty old boots,
the knockabout slouch hat?

And where was the constant cigarette in his
hand?

He was wearing pale moleskins, leather shoes
and a neat pale grey shirt—admittedly without a tie.
That would really be something—to see Tom
Scanlon in a tie. The shirt had a trendy Neru collar,
with the top button left undone. But only the top
button—not slashed open as so often in the past,
uncaringly showing an expanse of bronzed, muscular chest.

His hair, though still curly, still wild—nothing
could completely tame those unruly curls—now
barely reached the top of his collar. It was neatly
brushed back from his deeply tanned face, although
a wayward lock was already slipping forward over
his brow.

She swallowed, gathering her strength. 'Well…
Tom Scanlon.' Her tone was as withering as she
could make it. 'The man who decided marriage
wasn't for him.' *Or had his new girlfriend changed
his mind?*

'Tash—'

Tash. Her heart twisted, bitterness coiling

through her. Tom was the only one who'd ever called her that. It had been a special name…once. Now she couldn't bear to hear it.

'Don't you dare call me that!' She balled her hands into white-knuckled fists, her eyes spitting fire. 'I can't believe you have the nerve to come back and face me—as if nothing ever happened.' *Just when I was beginning to get over you…beginning to think I could survive without you.*

His chest expanded in a deep indrawn breath that hissed out through his teeth. 'A lot of water has flowed under the bridge since then, Ta—Natasha.'

There was to be no apology then, no begging for forgiveness. No…that wouldn't be Tom Scanlon's style. *Water under the bridge*…that was all the past eighteen months had been to him. She tilted her chin, the blue of her eyes turning to cold, glinting silver. No matter what it took, she wasn't going to show him how much he'd hurt her.

'Yes, one moves on,' she agreed coolly.

She didn't ask what he'd been doing with himself. He and his new love. Or if he was still in Sydney. Or what kind of work he'd taken on since tossing in his job as a helicopter pilot. Knowing Tom, he could turn his hand to just about anything. Before he'd become a pilot, he'd worked as a jackaroo, a horse-breaker, a dynamiter, a roof tiler, and heaven knew what else, but he'd never, as far as she knew, worked in a city office. He'd always preferred the outback, the wide open spaces. *Freedom...*

Had his new girlfriend tamed him enough to put him behind a desk? He had some accounting qualifications, he'd told her once, which would come in handy, he'd said, when he owned his own cattle station—his long-time dream.

A pipedream. A beautiful, remote pipedream.

She composed her face into a stony mask, to cover a surge of bitterness. Everything about Tom Scanlon had been a pipedream. Pie in the sky. Ambitious daydreams. Nothing he did or said or promised had been real. *When you find the love of your life, you want to seize her with both hands and never let her go,* he'd told her on the night he'd proposed.

Her heart wrenched at the thought of the love they'd shared; the laughter and the long talks about everything under the sun. Although their busy lives had kept them apart for much of their whirlwind two-month courtship, they'd been as close as any two people could be...or so she'd thought.

It had never struck her for a second that anything could ever come between them....

'A lot can happen in a year and a half,' Tom mused aloud. His eyes searched hers—or tried to. She snapped her gaze away before they could delve too deeply. 'I didn't just go off and forget you, Tash. I've been concerned about you.'

Concerned? How gullible did he think she was?

When she made no comment he didn't pursue it. 'I flew into Brisbane this morning,' he said conversationally. 'I wanted to see how you were doing. How your paintings were going. How life has been...treating you.'

And to find out if she was still pining for him; still heartbroken at losing him? Or if she'd managed to crawl out of her misery yet and find someone else...the way he had?

Ice clawed at her heart. Perhaps he would feel less guilty if she *had* taken up with another man, the way he'd taken up with—and presumably found happiness with—another woman. Or was he hoping she hadn't found anyone else? No doubt he'd get a the perverse satisfaction of assuming he was irreplaceable.

'Well, as you can see, I'm fine.' He didn't need to know any more than that. He didn't *deserve* to know. Let him stew. Let him wonder all he liked.

'That's good. I'm glad. You look great, Tash.' She felt his eyes rake over her, as hers had flicked over him a moment ago. It was such a searing scrutiny that she felt suddenly exposed and raw, as if his hot gaze was stripping her bare.

It made her feel self-conscious, uncomfortably aware of her paint-spattered smock, the frayed shorts underneath, the paint splodges on her bare legs and feet. Her own untidy mane of layered honey-blond hair was caught back in a black scrunchie, but long wisps had come loose and were trailing over her flushed cheeks and down her bare neck. And she had an uneasy feeling, as his piercing blue eyes came to rest on her face, that she had a dob of paint on the tip of her nose.

'I can do without the flattery, thanks,' she snapped, but her voice was lamentably unsteady. 'And I told you to stop calling me Tash!' Knowing what a sorry mess she must look made it even harder to accept his glib compliment. She wondered what the new woman in his life looked like…the irresistible siren who'd 'swept him off his feet', as he'd put it when he'd called her from Sydney to break off their engagement eighteen months ago.

The thought of his shock betrayal galvanised her into action. She tossed back her head, her gaze coldly scathing, showing none of the churning havoc behind, none of the harrowing emotions she'd buried for the past eighteen months and could now feel quivering to life again.

'Well, you've seen me now,' she scraped out. 'You've seen that I haven't slit my wrists or fallen in a heap. Now you'll have to excuse me, I'm busy. Charlie, would you see Tom out?' She had to get rid of her treacherous ex-fiancé before he realised what the sight of him was doing to her.

Her father sighed, and turned to Tom. 'Sorry, mate, it's a bad time. Nat's busy. Come on, I'll see you out.'

Mate? A bad *time?* Natasha glowered at her father. Traitor, she thought bitterly. Charlie had always liked Tom. Despite Tom's wild, rough-diamond looks and adventurous, freewheeling lifestyle, he'd taken to Tom like a house on fire, succumbing to the same irresistible macho charm that had demolished her own defences. Her father couldn't understand why they'd broken up so suddenly, when they'd appeared to be so crazy about each other.

She'd felt too hurt and humiliated to tell Charlie that Tom had fallen for another woman, and in the weeks and months that had followed their break-up she'd refused to mention Tom at all. She'd simply told her father what Tom had told *her* before she'd forced him into admitting he'd met someone else...that he'd decided he wasn't cut out for marriage after all and had wanted his freedom.

Tom began to leave, then paused, his gaze flicking to the painting on her easel. 'You've captured it perfectly,' he murmured. 'The spectacular colours at sunset...the clouds...the shadows. It's just as I remember it that evening.'

That evening... Her heart missed a beat. The reminder that he'd been with her the first time she'd watched the sun set over Ayers Rock brought bittersweet memories flooding back, sending deep tremors through her.

She'd been on a painting trip to the Red Centre, and Tom had been the helicopter pilot who'd flown her to Ayers Rock from Alice Springs. They'd clicked immediately, and for the next blissful two months they'd tried to see each other whenever they could. She'd been so sure they were soul mates, that they'd been meant for each other—two free spirits who'd answered a need in each other, who both wanted the same things…or so she'd thought.

But the dream had shattered when Tom had flown down to Sydney, telling her only that he had 'something to see to.' Within a week he'd phoned to tell her it was over and he'd met someone else.

'Is it for sale?'

Her head snapped back. He wanted to *buy* it? Did he have any idea what her paintings were worth these days? Her traditional Australian landscapes had really taken off in the past couple of years. They were in demand all over Australia. Even the Prime Minister had commissioned one, for Parliament House in Canberra. Her prices had soared as a result. Soared way out of Tom Scanlon's pocket…assuming he was still saving every cent he could scrape together to buy a cattle station one day. She couldn't imagine he'd have the spare cash to splash out on luxuries like original oil paintings.

Unless he'd abandoned his long-time dream since

taking up with his Sydney siren. *I need new challenges…a change of scene,* he'd told her back then. He'd already tossed in his job as a helicopter pilot, as if determined to cut his ties to the outback he'd always loved. She supposed it was possible he'd used his hard-earned savings to buy a swanky new city home for his new love and himself. A home he was now adorning with equally swanky paintings.

She dragged in a ragged breath. Where *was* the new woman in his life? Had Tom brought her here to Brisbane with him? Did his girlfriend have any idea he was making house calls on his ex-fiancée?

The questions were on the tip of her tongue, but she swallowed the urge to voice them aloud. She didn't want to show Tom that she was interested in his life any more. She wasn't!

'It's not for sale,' she said curtly. She'd done similar paintings of the Rock at sunset for an exhibition she'd held a few months ago, and they'd been snapped up immediately—every single one. She'd regretted seeing the last one go, and on an impulse had decided to paint another one to keep for herself. She wasn't sure quite why. She didn't even have a spare wall to hang it on. The gallery next door and the family apartment upstairs were already bursting at the seams.

She shifted restlessly. Maybe she wouldn't keep the painting after all. It would be too much of a reminder of a time she wanted to forget. She'd been mad to even consider keeping it and she'd have no trouble selling it. She could paint this scene over and over and sell every last one, no trouble at all.

But if she did put this one up for sale, she certainly wasn't going to sell it to Tom Scanlon. No way. It would be too humiliating, knowing he'd be sharing this once special scene, this once special evening, this one special moment in time, with the woman who'd replaced her.

'That's too bad.' Tom shrugged in a way that made her lips tighten. He was probably already regretting making the rash offer. He would hardly want to be reminded of that intoxicatingly romantic evening either.

Her eyes appealed to her father, and Charlie, with a rueful grimace, ushered Tom out at last. She averted her gaze, afraid that her eyes might reveal a yearning behind their steely coldness, a yearning she couldn't believe she could feel, after what he'd done to her.

Thank heaven she and her father were going away tomorrow on a two-week painting trip. There'd be no chance of running into Tom again, assuming he was staying in Brisbane for a few more days. More likely he'd be rushing back to Sydney on the first available flight—back to the more welcoming arms of the woman he'd preferred to her.

She couldn't settle down to work after he'd gone. She moved to the window and stood for timeless minutes staring out into the city street, trembling from the disturbing encounter. Unresolved questions swirled through her mind. Maybe it had been a mistake not asking Tom about the new woman in his life, and whether he'd found a city job and settled down in Sydney for good—or whether he'd been drawn back to his beloved outback. With her curiosity satisfied, she could have put him out of her mind, and out of her life, once and for all.

But it would have been unbearably painful to hear about his new love from Tom's own lips…to have to endure him extolling the virtues of the woman he hadn't been able to resist…*'I didn't mean it to happen, Tash,'* he'd said. *'It hit me like a bolt out of the blue.'*

It made her wonder if he had ever felt that way about *her*. A bitter glint lit her eyes. He'd certainly fooled her into thinking he had. *'I've found my soul mate in you, Tash… You and I were meant for each other… I never believed I could love as much…'*

But it still hadn't been enough. It had only taken a week in Sydney to—

She stiffened in disbelief. Tom Scanlon had appeared in her line of sight. He'd just emerged from the gallery and framing shop next door! She couldn't believe it. He hadn't left earlier, as she'd assumed. He'd been with her father in the gallery all this time!

Her eyes sparked with anger. How dare he hang

around her father after she'd ordered him to go!
How dare he soft-soap Charlie, after he'd failed to
melt *her!*

If Charlie's been talking to Tom Scanlon about
me, I'll kill him, she vowed. Whirling round, she
marched out of her studio and burst into the art
gallery next door. She found her father working on
a frame in the back room.

'What did you say to Tom Scanlon after he left
me?' she blazed. 'Why did he stay so long? You
know I didn't want him here. He's out of my life
now and I want him to stay out. Anyway, he's probably m-married by now to somebody else.'

'Married? What on earth makes you think that,
love? Tom wanted to be free, you told me. He'd
hardly rush off and marry someone else.'

'It's easier for a man to tell a girl he's not cut
out for marriage and wants his freedom,' Natasha
sneered, 'than to admit he wants to be free to play
around with other women!' No need to tell her father that Tom had already found someone else before he'd broken off their engagement. She didn't
want Charlie to start feeling sorry for her all over
again.

'Well? Why did he stay for so long?' she pressed.
'What did you talk about?' She wasn't quite sure
why she had to know.

'Tom just wanted to have a look around the gallery, that's all.' Was Charlie avoiding her eye? He'd

bowed his head over the frame he was working on and was frowning heavily, as if in concentration. 'As a matter of fact, he bought a painting,' he muttered, almost as an afterthought.

She blinked. So Tom had been serious about buying a painting. 'Which painting?' They didn't only hang her own paintings in the gallery. They displayed the paintings of several promising young Brisbane artists as well. Some of them were very good, yet their prices were still reasonable. Far cheaper than her own.

'One of yours.' Her father didn't look up. 'The one of the cherry blossom trees in the Botanical Gardens.'

Her jaw dropped. Why on earth would Tom Scanlon want to buy that particular painting? They'd once strolled arm in arm through the Gardens, admiring the spring blossom. They'd even kissed under those very same trees! Why in the world would he want to be reminded of it? It had been hard enough for her to go back to the Gardens last spring and paint there!

The painting for sale in the gallery had been one of her smaller works, a delicate watercolour, priced more reasonably than her larger oil paintings. Perhaps it had been the only painting of hers within Tom's means. But why buy one of her paintings at all?

Maybe because it was pretty, and he'd wanted a

romantic coming-home gift for his lover back in Sydney. But would Tom be that insensitive—to give his girlfriend a sentimental painting done by his ex-fiancée?

If he'd told her he *had* an ex-fiancée.

Her brow darkened. Nothing Tom Scanlon did made sense any more. He was no longer the man she'd known...or thought she'd known. Not that she cared what he did any more, or why he did any of the things he did. He was out of her life now.

'That's all? He just wanted to buy a painting? You didn't talk about anything else?' *Damn it, Natasha, you don't care, so why ask?*

Her father glanced up, his eyes bemused. 'If you had any questions for him, Nat, you had your chance to ask him face to face. It's not my business to ask him.'

'No, of course not.' Her chin lifted. 'And don't be silly, of course I don't have any questions I'd want to ask Tom Scanlon! I couldn't get rid of him quick enough—as you saw.' She realised she was shaking, not just her hands, but her whole body. Just as well she wasn't still trying to paint!

'Nat—' Charlie began, and seemed to hesitate. 'The very fact that he came back to see you shows that he must still care about you...that he's been thinking about you,' he amended, as pained eyes flew to his. 'He's had his freedom...eighteen months of it. He most likely has it out of his system by now. If you still care about him yourself—'

'I don't!' she cried, and bit her lip. 'Dad, you don't understand.' She was calling him Dad again, a sign of growing distress. She folded her arms to hide her trembling hands. 'He *hurt* me. I'm not going to let him hurt me again. I'm over him now and I don't ever want to see him again.'

Her father gave her a long searching look. 'Maybe I know you, Nat, better than you know yourself.'

'Oh, yes?' She glared at him indignantly But she could feel her lip wobbling.

'I think you do care, deep down. And I think he still cares too. Time's a great healer, Nat.'

'Dad…' She heaved a shuddering sigh. 'Forget it. There's not going to be a happy ending, so don't start dreaming of one. It's not going to happen. What we had once is dead and buried. He killed it. He—' She flicked her tongue over her lips. She would have to tell him. It was the only way he'd understand. 'He dumped me for someone else!'

It was out. Finally.

Her father's head shot up. She flinched at the rush of sympathy in his eyes. But the anger she expected to see wasn't there…the anger he should have been directing at Tom.

'Nat… I know it must have hurt you. But some men get cold feet at the thought of marriage, and panic. Maybe Tom just wanted an excuse to get away for a while…to be on his own. Or maybe he just needed some breathing space, and took up with someone else on the rebound—and later came to regret it and realise he'd made a terrible mistake. And now he's come back to find out if there's any hope of a second chance.'

'A second chance? Forget it!' She shot her father a quick, probing frown. 'Who says he regrets it?' she cracked out. 'Did he say anything about his—his girlfriend to you?'

'No,' Charlie admitted. 'But why would he come all the way here to see you, Nat, and want to buy one of your paintings, if he's still involved with someone else?'

'Oh, Dad, you're so naive. Because he feels *guilty*. Because his conscience is bothering him. He just wanted to check that I hadn't fallen into a black hole, so that he could get on with his life without feeling guilty any more. Well, I showed him.' She tossed her head. 'I showed him I'm well and truly over him.' A tremor shook through her. 'But there was no way I was going to be all chummy and forgiving. I wouldn't give him the satisfaction.'

'No…rightly so,' Charlie murmured, examining the frame in his hand. 'I'd better get on with this, Nat…I have to finish it before we leave tomorrow.'

She pursed her lips. He was taking Tom Scanlon's treachery very lightly. Obviously, her father was prepared to forgive and forget…without even knowing if Tom was still tied up with the woman he'd run away with. It defied belief!

'I've got things to finish this afternoon, too, and I've still got to pack,' she growled. 'I could have done without this interruption.' She scowled, still hovering, despite herself. 'Let's forget he ever came. All right?'

'Anything you say, love.'

She shot him a suspicious look. But Charlie's face was bland. Disturbingly bland.

Well, he could hardly be planning to invite Tom back for a return visit. Tomorrow Charlie was taking her up north on a painting trip. Her first ever trip to Kakadu National Park. She'd agreed to hold an exhibition of her paintings in Sydney in the spring, with Kakadu as her subject.

Kakadu was way up north, near Darwin, at the Top End of Australia. She'd be safe up there.

Safe from Tom Scanlon.

Perfectly safe.

CHAPTER TWO

WHEN she came into the kitchen the next morning to grab some coffee before the early morning flight to Darwin, Natasha found Aunt Edith, her father's widowed sister, already there. Edith was going to stay in their flat and look after the gallery and framing business while they were away up north. Since her husband's death last year, Edith had been helping out in the gallery part-time, and she often popped in to help with the cleaning and cooking, or to join them for a meal.

'Hi, Aunt Edith.'

'Good morning, dear.'

There was something about Edith's usually cheery greeting that alerted Natasha. 'Is something wrong, Auntie?' She frowned and glanced round. 'Where's Charlie?' Her father was usually up at the crack of dawn.

'Oh dear, your father's come down with the flu, dear. And to make matters even worse, he has gout in his big toe.'

'Oh, no!' On the very day they were planning to fly to Darwin! 'How bad is he? Have you called the doctor?' Sympathy for her father vied with dismay

24

at what it meant. She'd planned this Kakadu trip so carefully, deliberately choosing this time of year— early May, the start of the dry season, when the grass would still be green and the flowers still blooming. To postpone it, even for a couple of weeks, would upset her carefully-made plans and put her entire working schedule out in the coming months.

Edith grimaced. 'He wouldn't let me. He said the doctor would only tell him to stay in bed, and he's already *in* bed. Luckily he has tablets for his gout.' She seemed to hesitate. 'He demanded his mobile phone so that he could make some phone calls— the last thing he should be doing, the state he's in.' She sniffed her disapproval.

'I'll go and see him.' Chewing on her lip, Natasha darted off.

She expected her father to be sitting up in bed, propped up on pillows, or in an armchair with the mobile phone clamped to his ear, but he was lying in bed huddled under the blankets, with only the silvery top of his head showing and a big cage-like mound at the foot of the bed protecting his gouty foot. Her heart sank.

'Dad...'

He peeked up at her. 'Sorry, love, I'm sick. Really sick.' His voice was thin and wavery, his normally lively blue eyes half closed, as if it were an effort to keep them open. 'But you're not to worry, I've arranged everything. You're still to catch the plane at nine.'

'Oh, Dad, how can I go without *you?* I can't go camping for two weeks in Kakadu Park on my own! And at this late stage there's no one else I—'

'Love, I've fixed it, I said,' Charlie insisted weakly. 'I've contacted a safari tour company—'

'Dad, I'm not going on one of those organised tours—even if it's in a four-wheel-drive with only a handful of people. I want to be able to go where I like, when I like, and take as long as I need to get the shots and the sketches I want, and do the painting I want.'

'You'll still be able to do all that, love. The tour boss himself is going to take you—personally. I've checked him out and he's thoroughly reliable and highly regarded throughout the Top End. He'll take you wherever you want to go—and he'll see to all the food and help you put up your tent and lift any heavy gear for you and protect you from the crocodiles...' A weak smile flickered.

'Charlie—'

'He'll be waiting at Darwin airport to meet you, love, holding up a sign with your name on it. His name...now what was it? Cannon...something like that. He'll be wearing an insignia on his shirt and hat in the shape of a magpie goose, he said, with the name *Wild-Goose-Chase Tours* woven into it.'

'*Wild-Goose-Chase Tours?*'

'Neat name, huh? Attention grabbing. I told him you were a gorgeous blonde and that you'd be wearing a T-shirt with Monet waterlilies front and back. So make sure you're wearing it.'

'Oh, Dad.' She sighed. Sick as he was, Charlie appeared to have thought of everything. Luckily, her Monet shirt was clean. It was a favourite, and she'd already planned to take it with her. She would change into it after she'd finished her coffee. *If* she decided to go...

'Dad, you might be better in a couple of days...'

'I won't...and don't come near me! You don't want to catch it.' He waved her away with a feeble hand. 'Even if this rotten gout gets better in a few days, the flu's bound to develop into a shocking head cold, with an ear infection—it always does with me—and I won't be able to fly for weeks. But don't worry, I'll be fine, love,' he assured her hastily. 'Edith will look after me.'

'Dad—'

'You don't have to do a thing, love. I've already cancelled the four-wheel-drive we were planning to hire in Darwin. The tour company will provide one, as well as a tent and camping gear and all your food, etc. You just have to turn up. Now off you go and get ready.'

She knew he'd only get upset if she stood around arguing. 'Thanks, Dad.' She gave him a rallying smile. Sick as he was, he'd tried his best to put things right for her. The least she could do was sound grateful. 'I'll take my mobile phone to Darwin with me so we can keep in touch.'

He grunted. 'Don't waste your time making calls back home. You'll be out of range most of the time anyway. Besides, Edith says she's taking my phone away.' He sighed, a wavery sound. 'Sorry, love... I'm so tired.'

'Then go to sleep, Dad. And make sure you get Aunt Edith to call the doctor if you feel any worse.' She gave her father a pat—carefully avoiding the area of his feet. 'You take good care of yourself, Charlie. Get better soon.'

She couldn't believe that she was agreeing to go, that her father was actually *urging* her to go—to go careering off into the Australian wilds with a complete stranger. But if Charlie was happy for his daughter to go off on a two-week camping tour with a tour operator neither of them had met personally, he must be confident that the man was absolutely trustworthy.

This Cannon character, being the boss, and presumably the owner of Wild-Good-Chase Tours, was probably a mature, older man, married most likely, and he should at least be dependable and well experienced in the bush.

Besides, she had to go...people were depending on her. If she didn't come up with the paintings of Kakadu that she'd promised to produce by early spring, she might never be invited to exhibit in Sydney again! She'd be seen as unreliable, and her reputation in the art world would suffer.

She hurried back to the kitchen to grab a much needed cup of coffee.

As soon as she stepped out of the packed aircraft after the long flight north, the humid warmth in the air, the casual surroundings, and the people milling round the terminal in shorts and skimpy tops, confirmed that she was in Darwin. This was a city where things happened at a slower, easier pace, where people relaxed and enjoyed life.

Where most people relaxed, that was. Unless they were waiting to meet a complete stranger. A stranger who was going to be her close companion for the next two weeks—not in a civilised city with other people around, but alone in the bush, exploring Australia's largest, wildest and most exciting national park.

She gulped hard, and looked around for a man carrying a sign with her name on it. She could only see two people carrying signs, an elderly man and a young woman, and neither of their signs said Natasha Beale. And they weren't wearing insignias bearing the name *Wild-Goose-Chase Tours*.

She wasn't sure whether to wait, or go ahead and pick up her luggage. Maybe she'd find him there.

She could always call the tour company. As the boss he—

Her eyes widened. Her heart crashed against her ribs. A man was heading her way. A tall broad-shouldered man in knee-length khaki shorts, a dark shirt with an insignia on the pocket, and an Akubra hat with a similar badge…in the shape of a magpie goose, with the words *Wild-Goose-Chase Tours* clearly visible.

The man wasn't holding a card with her name on it. He didn't have to. He knew precisely who she was. Just as she knew who *he* was.

'Tom Scanlon,' she breathed in disbelief. With an effort she managed to stop her legs crumbling beneath her. That insignia on his cap…on his shirt… No, it wasn't possible! She could feel herself plunging into a nightmare. A nightmare her own *father* must have had a hand in!

Cannon, Charlie had slyly—cunningly—called him. Scanlon…Cannon…how *devious*.

'Natasha…how was the flight?' Tom held out both arms, as if about to grasp her shoulders and give her a welcoming kiss on the cheek—or on the lips!

She jerked back, out of his reach. 'What in the world do you think you're up to, Tom Scanlon? What sick game are you playing this time?'

'No game. I'm answering a call for help,' he said mildly. 'Your father's fallen ill, I was sorry to hear, and can't travel with you—and he appealed to me to come to your rescue.'

Her eyes flared, then narrowed. 'He *knew* you were working up here in Darwin?' Her head was still spinning. She could barely think.

'I mentioned it to him yesterday. Did he tell you I bought one of your paintings?'

If he thought he was going to soften her up that way, he was sadly mistaken. 'If you imagine I'm going anywhere with you, Tom Scanlon—'

'Look, you'd better pick up your luggage. We can argue on the way. Can I carry something for you?'

She had a tote bag and her camera slung over her shoulder. 'I can manage, thanks.' She had to think! She had to get out of this ghastly mess.

'If you say so.' He actually had the nerve to take her arm as he steered her away. She shook it off.

'I'm going back on the next plane,' she bit out. And when she got home she'd give her father a piece of her mind, sick or not. How dare he hire Tom Scanlon to look after her—and be so under-hand about it! The last man on earth she'd ever go on a camping tour with. Go anywhere with.

'After your father's gone to all this trouble for you?' Tom's eyes, deeply blue against the rich tan of his face, reproached her. 'Charlie told me he was desperate and didn't know who else to turn to. It was only natural he'd appeal to me—someone he knows—having learned only yesterday that I run adventure safaris out of Darwin…which I've been doing for the past year.'

He had? He couldn't have stayed long in Sydney…

'But *you* didn't have to volunteer to take me!'

'Sorry, ma'am, but I was the only operator available at such short notice. And your father was very relieved that you'd have someone you both know to take care of you—someone he can rely on.'

'*Rely* on? *You?*' She turned scathing eyes to his. When had she ever been able to rely on Tom Scanlon to take care of her? 'Oh, this is too much!' she burst out. 'You'll have to find someone else to take me—I don't care where from. I'm not going anywhere with you!'

'You'd prefer to go with a total stranger?'

'I thought I *was* going with a total stranger.'

'Ah, but your father knew that you weren't. He knew you'd be safe with me. You will, Natasha,' Tom assured her seriously. 'This is a business arrangement, pure and simple. I'm just your driver…your guide…your minder, if you like. I'll be there to give you a helping hand and generally watch over you. This trip's obviously important to you. Let's make the best of it.'

The best of it? How could there be any 'best' about it, if *he* was involved? She inhaled a fraught breath. She could feel a net tightening around her.

But she wasn't going to meekly give in. 'You can answer some questions before I even think about it!'

'By all means…but we'd better grab your luggage first. Can you see your bag?'

Luggage was already revolving on the carousel, with people dashing forward to retrieve their bags.

Natasha spied her battered suitcase. It had been on many trips with her, usually around Queensland in her father's sturdy four-wheel-drive. If they'd had the time to spare they would have driven all the way to Kakadu instead of flying, but it would have added days, or even weeks, to the trip.

And what if her father had fallen ill on the way? It would have been a disaster!

'It's that one.' She dashed forward to snatch it up, but Tom was there before her, lifting the bag with ease. She had to admire his strength. The suitcase held not only heavy boots and all the clothes and toiletries she'd need for two weeks, but a first aid kit, a torch, films and equipment for her camera, her sketching and painting gear, and maps and compasses.

'Anything else?' Tom asked.

'A sleeping bag.' She'd decided to bring her own. 'There it is!'

He was there before her again, grabbing the rolled-up sleeping bag and slinging it over his shoulder. 'That it? Right. My four-wheel-drive's in the car park. I've already stocked up on food and drink. Anything else you want before we head off?'

He was assuming she'd already given in. *Had* she?

'I'll want a tent.' The answer popped out. If she was going to go anywhere with Tom Scanlon, she intended to have a tent all to herself. A two-man tent for reasonable comfort. Tom could provide his own tent—or sleep under the stars.

'No problem. I've a tent in the car.'

'I'll want a tent to myself.'

'You can have it. I always sleep out—except in the wet season, when I usually bunk down in the back of the four-wheel-drive.' He swung round, heading for the exit, expecting her to follow.

'Wait!' She didn't move. 'You said you'd answer some questions first.'

There was one question in particular that she had to know the answer to before she took another step.

'Sure.' He paused, turning his head. 'Fire away.' His eyes were unreadable under his slouch hat.

'Did you tell your girlfriend that you intend to go on a camping trip with your ex-fiancée?' She kept her tone cool, her expression as inscrutable as his. 'Or is she your wife now?'

It seemed an age before he answered. The answer came with a shrug. 'That didn't work out.' There was no emotion in his voice…no regret, no sadness,

no relief—nothing. Just a coolly impassive state-
ment of fact.

If he'd shown some feeling…

Bitterness rose like bile in her stomach. 'She left
you? Or did you leave her? You're good at that.
Leaving the women in your life.' She could have
bitten out her tongue the second the bitter words
were out. If he thought she still cared…still reacted
to him…still had feelings for him…

I don't! she told herself, tossing back her head,
her eyes turning to glinting ice. 'Forget it, I'm not
interested.' But under her cool-eyed unconcern, her
mind was reeling, her insides churning. So the irresistible *femme fatale* who'd struck him 'like a bolt
out of the blue' was no longer in the picture. It
hadn't worked out.

So much for his grand passion.

Her lip twisted. Had he tired of her, the way he'd
tired of his fiancée after an engagement of only two
weeks? He'd called *her* the light of his life once!
She scowled. Had he suffered cold feet all over
again at the thought of settling down? At the
thought of marriage?

She flounced past him. She didn't want to think
about it! 'Well, come on. Since I've little choice,
let's go.'

'No more questions?' As he caught up with her,
in a couple of long strides, his body language appeared more relaxed than it had been a second ago.

She'd seen how he'd tensed under her lashing scorn, flinching as she'd taunted him about leaving the women in his life.

'I haven't taken up with anyone else, if that's of any interest,' he assured her with the glimmer of a smile.

She shot him a look of searing contempt. 'It isn't. Your business is yours and mine is mine.' She kept her tone clipped, her eyes remote. 'Let's keep it that way.' If she was going to go on this camping trip with him, she had to keep it on a strictly business footing or she'd never survive a day with him, let alone two weeks. 'As you pointed out, this will be purely a business arrangement. Simply that.'

'Yes, ma'am.'

They reached his huge dust-covered four-wheel-drive without any further verbal clashes, sticking to safe subjects such as food, drinks, and other camping needs, all of which Tom had already packed into the vehicle. He appeared to have thought of everything.

'Have you had lunch?' he asked as he unlocked the big four-wheel-drive and heaved her suitcase and sleeping bag into a rear seat. With two rows of spare seats behind the two front seats, there was ample storage space.

'Yes, thank you, I had it on the plane.'

'Good, then we can head off straightaway. We'll

reach Kakadu Park by late afternoon.' He waved her in.

As she hauled herself up into the front passenger seat, she noticed an aluminium boat on the roof-rack above. An excited quiver ran through her. Having a boat at her disposal when they reached the Kakadu wetlands would give her far greater flexibility than a tourist boat cruise could ever provide.

But they'd have to be careful! Crocodiles abounded in the Yellow Water Billabong and the Alligator River system.

She smiled at the misnomer. She'd been reading up on Kakadu and knew that the South, West and East Alligator Rivers had been mistakenly named, since there were no alligators in Australia! The original explorer had seen the smaller freshwater crocodiles and mistaken them for the alligators he'd seen in North America. He'd obviously never seen a mighty twenty-foot-long man-eating saltwater crocodile!

'That's better,' Tom commented from the driver's seat.

Her head swung round. 'What's better?'

'You're smiling.' His lip quirked. 'At least you were,' he drawled as her smile vanished, her eyes clouding.

'I'm just keen to get going,' she said fractiously. 'I can't wait to see Kakadu.' She had to concentrate on that—on her reason for coming on this trip—and put everything else out of her mind!

'You're the boss. Like a drink of water before we set off?' Now that they were out of the comparatively cool terminal, the May sun was scorching, the humidity oppressive. 'It's important not to get dehydrated up here. It'll be even more vital once we hit Kakadu.'

'Okay. Thanks.'

Tom reached behind him to delve into a battery-operated refrigerator. He pulled out a bottle of water and handed it to her. While she was sipping, he grabbed another bottle for himself and gulped down several huge swallows.

'Ah, that's good,' he muttered, wiping a hand across his lips.

Her eyes widened. He'd once been a soft drink addict who always had a can of Coca-Cola or Pepsi in his hand, seldom plain water. Or if not a soft drink, a cold beer. *Water's boring*, he'd said, adding with a cheeky grin, *like most things that are good for you.*

She glanced away, compressing her lips at the memory. He must have found *her* boring too. He wouldn't have walked out on her otherwise...

'Keep your water bottle handy,' Tom advised, 'and take a swig as you need it.' He tucked his own bottle into the gap between the seats.

As they sped east along the Arnhem Highway,

Natasha sat tensely, staring straight ahead—not just to avoid Tom's eye, but because she was keen not to miss a thing, even though it would be another two-and-a-half hours before they reached Kakadu.

With light traffic and no speed limit in the Northern Territory, the big four-wheel-drive barrelled along the excellent bitumen highway. After a while she settled back in her seat, but she didn't relax. She couldn't. She was still trembling with anger and shock at the impossible situation she'd found herself in. If Tom had been safely married, or had still been with his girlfriend—still devoted to his girlfriend—she would have known how to treat him. She might even have been able to relax a little, knowing the past was well and truly buried and that she was safe from him.

But he was still free. Still unmarried.

Still the roving-eyed Romeo?

She steeled her heart. If he even thought of making another play for *her* after what he'd done to her already—if he dared try anything at *all*—she would push him into the nearest river and leave him to the crocodiles!

As they crossed the Marrakai Plains and the Adelaide River, Tom gave a running commentary, pointing out anything of special interest. Determined not to show any reaction to him, she buried her antagonism—for now—and asked the occasional question, even offering a few coolly interested comments. But as the kilometres rolled by, she couldn't prevent a sigh slipping from her lips.

'The bushland along here is pretty monotonous, I'm afraid,' Tom murmured, noting her sigh and mistaking it for boredom. 'Everyone finds the long drive to Kakadu a bit tedious. After being in the air all morning and driving all afternoon, I guess you'll be wanting to crash into bed early tonight.'

Bed! Heat flamed along her cheekbones. She wasn't ready to spend a night alone in the wilds with Tom Scanlon! She wasn't ready to camp out in the solitary bush with her ex-fiancé, sharing meals and an intimate camp fire, with no one else within miles, perhaps. She gave a faint shudder. But what choice did she have? She'd committed herself now.

'How does the idea of a real bed sound?'

Her head whipped round, her eyes wary. 'What are you talking about?'

'We have to go to the park headquarters at Jabaru to pick up our permits. How about I book us into the Crocodile Hotel just for tonight? My shout. We can have a good dinner there too. I think you deserve one civilised night before we trundle off into the wilds for two weeks.'

She inhaled a deep breath. It was tempting...if only to put off the inevitable. A comfortable night's sleep in the privacy of her own room would help to steel herself for the long nights she'd be camping out under the stars with her ex-fiancé—and the long days she'd have him breathing down her neck.

'Don't be silly, I wouldn't let you pay for me,' she hedged. 'A night at the Crocodile Hotel, with dinner, would cost you a fortune.' Tom had never splashed his money around. He'd *saved* it. At least he had…once. 'If I did agree to stay there, I'd pay for myself.' Luckily she'd brought a credit card with her.

'Let's find out if they've a room available first. Sorry—two rooms,' Tom corrected as her horrified gaze flew to his. He was swinging the big vehicle off the road as he spoke. 'I'll let you stretch your legs and take a close-up look at those giant ant-hills over there while I put a call through. And you'd better have some water—you're not drinking enough.' He'd been taking regular swigs from his own bottle, she'd noticed, as they'd been driving along.

She felt his eyes on her as he killed the engine. Glancing round at him as she took a few gulps from her water bottle, she saw a crooked smile on his lips.

'Very nice,' Tom murmured, an approving gleam in his deep blue eyes.

Her breath hissed in sharply, her eyes snapping in disbelief. He was staring—staring openly—at the swell of her *breasts!*

'Nice?' she echoed icily. If he was going to start

making sleazy comments, she was off! She would hire another four-wheel-drive and another guide—from somewhere. Jabaru, maybe. Any stranger would be preferable to this—this—

'Your T-shirt,' Tom said glibly. 'Very pretty. You like waterlilies?'

Her breath puffed out, her cheeks flaming as her anger deflated. He was admiring her Monet T-shirt!

'Yes, I…they…they're beautiful,' she stammered, feeling a complete fool.

'That they are.' His gaze was still on her T-shirt—quite unnecessarily now, she thought, her flush deepening. 'Well, you'll see plenty of water lilies on the flood plains,' he drawled. 'At Yellow Waters and other billabongs.'

'Yes…' she swallowed. 'I know. I intend to paint them.'

'I guessed you would.' He looked amused, damn him. He *knew* what she'd thought! 'We'll take our own boat out, rather than joining one of the tourist boats, and you'll be able to take all the time you like.' He pulled out his mobile phone. 'Well…I'd better make that call.'

It was a relief when his gaze left her burning face.

Grabbing her camera, she stepped out, taking a few hefty gulps of air as she turned away from the vehicle. The heat and humidity were intense but she barely noticed, her artist's eye captured by the huge rock-hard termite mounds standing like ancient fortresses in the drying grassland beside the road.

'Wow,' she whispered. To think that tiny ants had built these giants! They were awesome—worthy of a painting. She took photographs from various angles, then pulled out a small notebook and made a few pencil sketches, with notes.

Tom joined her a few minutes later. 'We're booked in,' he said, and paused, his eyes dancing. 'So now you can relax.' The corner of his lip quirked, as if he'd sensed her apprehension and was tickled by it. 'You'll be able to get a good night's sleep.'

'Great.' She intended to. 'Well, are you ready to go? The sooner we're there, the sooner I can get to—' she nearly said *bed*, but prudently avoided the word '—to sleep!'

Once back in the car and on their way, she realised she actually did feel more relaxed. Staying overnight at a civilised hotel would be a welcome reprieve.

An extravagant reprieve, she thought with a faint twinge of guilt.

Well…what the heck? What was a little extravagance, once in a while? She'd always wanted to see the famous hotel that was built in the shape of a crocodile.

CHAPTER THREE

THEY made one more stop on their way to Kakadu,
to have afternoon tea at a rustic roadside café.
Natasha chose an iced cinnamon bun from a selec-
tion of pastries and cakes, and a cup of tea. Tom
surprised her by ignoring the cakes and buying a
rosy red apple for himself.

As she watched him take a bite a question leapt
out. 'You're eating apples now? You always hated
apples. Chocolate bars were more your thing.'

She coloured, mentally kicking herself. Damn!
Why had she reminded him of the past—their past
together?

Tom shrugged, his lips curving in the kind of grin
that had once melted every bone in her body. 'I
never realised how delicious apples were until I
tried one.'

She twitched a shoulder and turned away, tightening her lips as she headed for a table, wondering
who'd managed to persuade him to try his first apple. The woman he'd ditched her for? She set her
cup down with a clatter, spilling tea into her saucer.

Tom didn't join her at the table. 'I'll be out in

44

the garden, stretching my legs. Join me when you're ready.'

Her eyes followed him as he strode off. Maybe that was how he'd managed to trim down so much—by exercising instead of sitting around all day in a four-wheel-drive, or a helicopter before that. And by eating fruit instead of cakes and chocolates, and drinking water instead of beer and sugary soft drinks. Had his girlfriend teased him about his weight? Nagged him into changing his bad habits?

She heaved a wobbly sigh. She'd never complained about the way Tom had looked herself. She'd loved him just as he was. Perhaps she should have. He looked terrific. A brand-new man. He'd always been a sexy, impressive-looking guy, but now he looked fantastic—a thousand times fitter and sexier than he'd been eighteen months ago.

Interesting lines slashed his cheeks, where before they'd verged on chubby. His jaw, previously masked by a bushman's beard, was square, strong and sharply defined. With his new streamlined frame, there was a new athletic swing in his step. A dynamic, virile energy—a revitalised energy—pulsated from him in waves.

This man, with his sexy new look, was pure dynamite!

In more ways than one. And she'd better remember it. Dynamite was dangerous. It could be deadly. He'd already destroyed her once.

She bit into her iced bun, resolutely blotting his potent image from her mind.

As they drove on, she kept her mind strictly on the passing scene, though there was little to see but endless eucalyptus and grasses, sprinkled with Pandanus, or screw palms, which the Aborigines, she'd read, put to good use, weaving the leaves into baskets and hats and eating the seeds from inside the woody fruit.

As they passed through the Kakadu entry station, Tom waved a hand to the surrounding bushland. 'You're seeing it at a good time—the grass is still green and there are flowers to give splashes of colour. It'll be brown and bone dry here in a few weeks.'

'That's why I wanted to come now,' Natasha said tightly. *It's the only reason I agreed to come with you,* her eyes told him. After falling silent for a few minutes she asked curiously, 'Are there many animals here in the woodlands? I've seen a few birds, but not a single animal.'

'You're unlikely to spot them in the heat of the day, let alone from a moving car, but they're there, never fear—especially round the waterholes and springs.'

'What sort of animals?'

'Oh, kangaroos, wallabies, lizards, possums,

sugar gliders, skinks, quolls, snakes…maybe even the odd crocodile.' He flicked her a look, as if expecting her to squeal or shudder. 'And birds galore. Once we start camping out you'll see what I mean.'

Once we start camping out… But they wouldn't be camping out tonight. Natasha blew out a shaky breath, feeling a mixture of relief and regret.

As they drove deeper into the park, she felt her heartbeat quicken, excited goose bumps shivering across her skin.

This was the real Australia, the ancient Australia, relatively untouched by modern civilisation. The Aboriginal people had lived at Kakadu—an area about the size of Wales—for over fifty thousand years, and they still lived here, as managers of the park; working as rangers, guides, artists, and protectors of the famed Aboriginal rock art, and in the tourist shops and cultural centres.

'Look…you can see the Escarpment now.' Tom was peering straight ahead, indicating the rugged sandstone cliffs rising from the bushland, dividing Kakadu from the Arnhem Land Plateau. 'We'll be at Jabaru shortly. We'll go straight to the hotel,' he decided. 'It's been a long day for you. You'll want to freshen up before dinner.'

She jerked upright, her mind leaping ahead. An intimate, leisurely dinner with Tom Scanlon in a four-star hotel restaurant, possibly with romantic music in the background, was the last thing she felt like facing tonight. If the hotel provided room service, she decided, she would have it in her room. Alone.

Besides, she had nothing suitable to wear to a classy restaurant. She'd brought only knockabout camping gear with her.

As they drove into the small township of Jabaru, Tom pointed out the swimming pool and the shopping centre. 'If there's anything you've forgotten, there's a supermarket—and a bank, if you need money.'

Did *he* need money, Natasha wondered, to pay for this extravagant night of luxury and comfort ahead?

Tom swung his four-wheel-drive into the tree-lined car park of the famed Gagudju 'Crocodile' Hotel, nosing the big vehicle into one of the circular parking bays—representing clutches of crocodile eggs! The giant crocodile-shaped hotel loomed alongside.

'Those huge legs on either side are the stairwells,' Tom explained as they pulled out their bags and cameras and headed for reception—which was inside the jaws of the crocodile. 'And the two big eyes on top are ventilators, and glow at night.'

As soon as she stepped into the spacious oasis-style reception area, Natasha realised that her argument about having nothing to wear to dinner wouldn't stand up. Everyone was dressed casually and lightly—this was the steamy outback, after all, even though it was pleasantly cool in the hotel. She had a feeling that few guests would doll themselves up for dinner.

She would just have to plead tiredness—after first checking if room service was available.

As they approached the reception desk, she hissed at Tom, 'I'll check myself in first.' She didn't want him giving the receptionist the impression that they were 'together' and needed adjoining rooms—or even a shared room, heaven forbid. Or that Tom was going to pay for her.

'Natasha Beale,' she said with a smile. 'My tour guide, Tom Scanlon, booked two rooms, I believe. We'll be paying separately.' Making their relationship perfectly clear—tour guide and tourist.

After being checked in and allocated her room, she asked the receptionist, 'Do you provide room service here—if I want dinner in my room?'

As the receptionist nodded, Tom shifted closer. 'Hey…you don't want to do that,' he drawled in an undertone. 'Be sociable. You've been shut up in the car all day.'

She flicked him a frown. 'I'm tired,' she gritted. 'I just want to crash. I'll see you in the morning, Tom. Say, around seven? I'd like to head off early, before it gets too hot.' With her room key in one hand, her bag in the other, and her camera slung over her shoulder, she stalked off, leaving Tom to do his own checking in.

As she climbed the stairs to the first floor, Tom's comment niggled at her. Dinner in the restaurant, with other people around, probably *would* be more pleasant than room service.

But to sit at an intimate table for two with Tom Scanlon… It would bring back so many bittersweet memories. The last time she and Tom had shared an intimate dinner together was the night he'd proposed. She squeezed her eyes shut, blotting out the poignant images of that blissfully romantic evening.

She dumped her gear, kicked off her shoes and just as she was inspecting her tastefully furnished room, she heard a knock at her door. Her heart jumped. It couldn't be Tom. Not this quickly. It must be one of the staff. Someone wanting to turn down her bed, maybe.

She pulled open the door.

Tom Scanlon filled the gap. He still had his bag on his shoulder. She tensed, but he made no attempt to step into the room. He just stood in the open doorway with his shoulder leaning against the door frame, looking down at her with a quizzical expression, his eyes deeply blue in his tanned face.

'Do you hate me that much, Natasha?'

Her eyebrows shot up—even as her stomach lurched.

'Excuse me?' she asked, feigning a coolness she

didn't feel. So much for keeping things business-like!

The corner of his lip lifted in an ironic smile. 'You can't even bear to have dinner with me?' He gave a shake of his head, his eyes mocking her. 'How are you going to survive the next two weeks if you can't even face up to having a civilised meal in a hotel restaurant with me?'

I don't know, she wanted to shout back. *I honestly don't know!*

This was the very thing she'd wanted to avoid at all cost—allowing their personal differences to intrude. And she'd brought it on herself!

'Don't take it personally.' She tossed back silken wisps of honey-gold hair. 'Just because I'd prefer room service to dining in public, doesn't mean I'm avoiding having dinner with you.' *Liar*, she thought, gulping. 'I'm just dog-tired, that's all. I simply don't have the energy to tizzy myself up and appear all bright and bushytailed for a restaurant full of people.'

'This is Kakadu Park, not the Ritz, Ta—Natasha.' The crooked smile curved a bit more. 'I reckon, if you had a long hot shower and put your feet up for an hour, you'd feel a thousand times better. There's plenty of time. You don't need to dress up for dinner. A clean shirt and a pair of jeans will do fine. Don't even bother about make-up—you're lucky, you don't need it.'

Natasha opened her mouth, then shut it again. Why bother arguing? Sighing, she gave in with a shrug. 'Very well…as long as you remember our bargain. This trip is strictly business. I'm here to paint and you're here to drive and protect me from crocodiles.' Her eyes glinted a challenge. 'We go halves with the bill. And over dinner we stick to talking about our trip. Or the weather. Or the state of the nation. Anything but—' she sucked in her breath. Even to say the words was likely to inflame the situation.

But Tom said them anyway. 'Anything but us?' He looked down at her for a deep searching moment. 'So it's not so much hate…as fear,' he murmured, arching an eyebrow.

She gaped at him. '*Fear?* You think I'm *afraid* of you? You must be off your head!'

'Maybe not afraid of *me*…no,' he conceded. 'More…afraid of something in yourself. Afraid that you might still have some feelings. Feelings you don't want to have.'

'*Feelings?* For *you?* Oh, you sure have tickets on yourself!' She turned on him then, her eyes spitting silver fire. 'I'll tell you what I feel. *Nothing.* Understand? I don't feel hate or fear or hurt or anger or anything at all. Any feelings I had for you, Tom Scanlon, died long ago.' Her chest heaved, her breath coming in furious gulps. 'Sorry, but as far as you're concerned, I feel nothing at all!'

She moaned inwardly as she listened to herself. Why was she getting so steamed up, if she felt nothing?

'Okay, okay, my mistake.' Tom held up his hands in surrender—the hands, she thought unsteadily, that had once roamed all over her body…the hands that he'd loved to rake through her long hair…the hands that had once held her close and made her feel loved and safe.

Loved and safe? She shivered, and stepped back, the glint of cold pewter in her eyes. She'd never been loved and she'd never been safe. Not with Tom Scanlon. She'd been a fool to put her blind trust into a man she'd only known for two months— a good part of that time spent apart, thanks to Tom's hectic flying schedule. She'd seen him as the man of her dreams and he'd turned out to be a fickle, heartless cheat. It had taken him less than a week with another woman to show her how disgustingly fickle and heartless he was.

She felt Tom's eyes on her and jutted her chin, hardening her heart as she met his searching blue gaze. If he thought that her outburst a moment ago meant that she still had some feelings for him, he was mightily mistaken.

'I'd like to have a rest now,' she jerked out, reaching for the door, ready to shut him out. 'And I want to put a call through to my father.'

'Ah, yes, poor old Charlie. Send him my best,

won't you? And try not to berate the poor guy for calling on me in your hour of need. Remember how sick he is.'

'Oh, I remember only too well,' she muttered. 'I'll meet you in the restaurant,' she added brusquely, not wanting to walk down the stairs with him, like a couple.

Perversely, she was almost beginning to look forward to the evening ahead now. It would be far better to front up to dinner looking cool and fresh and uncaring, than to hide herself away in her room and let him think that she couldn't face him.

'What time?' she rapped out.

'How about seven-thirty? That'll give you oodles of time for a rest and a freshen up, and it'll give me time to drive over to Park Headquarters and pick up our permits.'

Permits were required in certain areas, and when camping out overnight on a bush walk.

'Fine,' she said. 'See you at dinner.' She closed the door on him. Only to freeze a moment later, her nerve-ends springing upright as she heard the door of the room next door slam shut, and the sound of a bag being dropped on the floor. Tom had been given the room next door to hers!

She began to tremble, indignation mingling with anger—and a simmering apprehension. Had he *asked* for the room next door to hers? Would she have the *nerve?*

She blew out a sigh. Tom Scanlon, she thought darkly, would be capable of anything.

CHAPTER FOUR

By SEVEN-TWENTY, she was on her way down to the restaurant. She wanted to be safely seated at a table before Tom joined her. It was silly, she knew, but it would help to maintain some distance between them, walking in on her own. Affirming her independence.

Her steps faltered as she saw Tom waiting outside the restaurant. He was early! Tom Scanlon had never been early in his life…not in her experience, at any rate. He hated waiting around, doing nothing, wasting precious time.

Back in his days as a helicopter pilot, mustering cattle and flying tourists to the outback's top scenic spots, he'd always done things at a frenetic pace, always keeping himself busy until the last possible moment before rushing to meet her—arriving on time if he was lucky, but more likely running late.

There was no sign of restlessness or impatience in him now, as far as she could see. He looked more relaxed and laid-back than she'd ever seen him. What had made him change so much? Giving up his once burning ambition to buy a cattle station one day—as he appeared to have done—so that he was no longer in a mad rush to take on every well-paying job he could find to make as much money as he could, in the shortest possible time?

She could feel his eyes on her as she approached. Taking a deep breath, she made an effort to maintain her composure—even though the sight of him didn't help. He looked fresh and clean and breathtakingly sexy. He was no longer wearing the dark tour shirt and shorts, or the wide-brimmed hat and heavy boots. He was wearing a light-coloured shirt, open at the throat—she hastily averted her gaze—with long pants and a clean pair of boots. He'd obviously just had a shower—his curly hair was still damp, and freshly combed back.

Before she could find her voice, he commented with a slow grin, 'Well, the rest seems to have done you a power of good, Miss Beale. You look a million dollars.' Teasing eyes met hers. 'Sorry…am I allowed to say that?'

Her eyes didn't even waver—though it took quite an effort. 'Thank you,' she said graciously, accepting the compliment as she would from any politely friendly tour guide. Yet deep down she was glad she'd made an effort, glad she'd chosen a crisp white shirt and her clean buff-coloured jeans, and had taken some care with her hair. But she'd done it for herself—to perk *herself* up—not for him!

She even flashed him a cool smile. Again, it was not for him, but for herself. It was a long time since she'd cared how she looked. Since Tom had walked out of her life no man had stirred her enough to want to make a special effort. Being told she looked 'a million dollars,' even if it was shallow flattery, just to make her feel better, somehow *did* make her feel better. More in control. Better able to get through the evening ahead.

'I'm hungry, are you?' She waved a careless hand. 'Let's go in.'

The restaurant, in keeping with the spirit of Kakadu, had ochre-coloured walls, timber-topped tables and even a crocodile carpet! After they were seated, a young drinks waitress appeared. Natasha ordered a glass of mineral water, and was surprised when Tom did too.

'With ice and lemon please,' he requested. When the two tall glasses arrived, Tom raised his and let it hover between them. 'Cheers,' he said with a coaxing half-smile.

'Cheers,' she returned, determined to be pleasant. Pleasant, yet serenely indifferent. She watched as he took a long deep sip. He was certainly taking the hot tropical climate seriously—quenching his thirst with water rather than a cold beer, as he would have in the past.

Or was he simply watching his weight? Having reached his present stunning shape and fitness—the toned muscles, the lean lines, the flat stomach—she guessed that he'd hardly want to go back to the overweight, chain-smoking giant he'd been before.

She pursed her lips. She hadn't seen a cigarette in his hand, she realised, since they'd met up again.

Curiosity won over discretion. 'You've given up smoking?' she asked. Most people put weight *on* when they gave up smoking. Tom had only become more streamlined.

'Well over a year ago. Are you proud of me?' he asked, his eyes flickering with a warmth that brought an unwanted flutter—and a surge of anger that curled her hands into fists. He actually expected her to be *proud* of him? It would take a miracle— a couple of lifetimes—to make her proud of *any-thing* her traitorous ex-fiancé did!

She began to study her menu with an intent frown, not bothering to answer.

'Do you still prefer white wine?' Tom asked. He was consulting the wine list. 'Or would you rather have red?'

Her eyelashes fluttered upward. At least he wasn't blithely assuming that she would still have the same likes and dislikes as eighteen months ago…that she wouldn't have changed since the day he'd walked out of her life.

'White, thanks,' she said, adding coolly, 'Just one glass will do for me.' She wanted to keep a clear head.

'I'll have white too,' Tom drawled. 'Chardonnay okay?'

'Fine.'

Instead of ordering a bottle of wine he surprised her yet again by ordering two glasses of the chardonnay. Never before had she known Tom Scanlon to order a single glass of wine for himself, rather than a whole bottle—which he'd never had any trouble polishing off in the past, with or without her help.

'Are you ready to order?' A waitress hovered over them.

Natasha nodded. 'I'll have the marinated crocodile, thanks, as an entrée.' She could hardly come to Kakadu without trying crocodile! 'And kangaroo as a main course,' she said, wanting to stick to indigenous foods—the restaurant's speciality.

Tom looked up from his own menu. 'I'll have the Caesar salad, followed by the grilled barramundi, thanks. With the steamed vegetable basket.'

'Would you like a bowl of French fries with your fish, sir?'

'Just the vegetables, thanks.'

Natasha's eyes snapped to his. He was refusing *French fries?*

Tom gave a low chuckle as the waitress melted away. 'If you could have seen your face a second ago! I'm a constant surprise to you, aren't I, Natasha? No cigarettes, no chocolate bars, no beer, no French fries. What next, you must be wondering?'

Her eyebrows shot up. 'I assure you, I'm not wondering anything of the sort.' *Oh, no?* 'So…' A cynical twist curved her lip. 'You've changed your bad habits. Congratulations. What do you want, a medal?'

'No, I don't want a medal.' Tom's tone sobered, his blue eyes clouding. 'I want…' He paused. 'I just want us to be friends again, Tash. It would make the next two weeks so much easier. For both of us.'

'Then don't call me Tash!' she bit back. It brought back too many memories. Too many intimate, heart-tugging memories. Memories that no longer had any meaning or substance. Memories that had long since turned to dust and ashes.

Tom inclined his dark head. 'Sorry. Natasha.' He raised his glass of wine. 'To you.'

She shrugged, trying not to react to him as she took a sip of her wine. 'Very nice,' she muttered, and straightened her shoulders with new determination as she met his whimsical blue gaze. 'I know you're dying to tell me what brought about all these amazing lifestyle changes…so tell me,' she invited coolly. Maybe, if she showed him that she was willing to hear about the past eighteen months, she could convince him it no longer affected her.

And convince herself at the same time.

She could tell by the wavering of his eyes and

the swell of his chest as he inhaled a deep breath, that she'd surprised *him* this time. He hadn't expected her to quiz him. She could see him hesitating, could sense his mind ticking over, as if he wasn't sure how to tell her. Or didn't *want* to tell her.

Her heart hardened. Because the past eighteen months were all tied up with that other woman? Or other women? She drew in her lips, her eyes smouldering under her thick lashes. No wonder he was hesitating. He wouldn't want to open up the old wounds again and expose the bitterness that still festered below. And she'd be mad if she dragged the sordid details out of him.

She opened her mouth to tell him she wasn't really interested, but he spoke first.

'My father died a few months ago.' She heard emotion in his voice for the first time…emotion for the father he'd seldom mentioned and hadn't seen for years, as far as she knew. 'He was only sixty-four. My mother, as you might remember me telling you, died at fifty-one. And an uncle died far too soon too, after years as an invalid. It hit me suddenly how short life can be. It did something to me, woke me up to what I was doing to myself. I realised I'd have to do something or *I'd* be unlikely to see old age either. Certainly not a healthy old age.'

Natasha sat very still. Something in his voice was threatening to unravel the protective web she'd wound round her heart. For the first time since she'd known him, Tom Scanlon was showing a raw, sensitive, vulnerable side. Showing he wasn't invincible…and that he'd finally come to realise it. The death of his parents and uncle had woken him up to the destructive path he'd been following.

It hadn't been his girlfriend's teasing or nagging that had made him change his bad habits. It was the premature death of his loved ones, forcing the decision on him, to avoid a similar fate.

'I'm sorry to hear about your father, Tom,' she said, and had to clear her throat. She'd never met his father, and Tom had never wanted to talk about him. *We didn't get on*, was about all he'd ever said. His father had remarried after Tom's mother died, and Tom hadn't hit it off with his new stepmother either. He'd left home after a blazing row, and he and his father hadn't spoken since. End of subject, as far as Tom had been concerned.

'Thanks,' Tom said, and again she sensed that he was trying to suppress some deeply felt emotion, even though his face was impassive, his blue eyes hooded, as if he were wary of more questions. But she asked anyway.

'Did you…have a chance to see your father before he died?' she ventured. *Did you have a chance to reconcile?* was what she meant.

Tom shook his head. 'I'm afraid not.' He was looking down at his glass now, a muscle twitching at his temple. 'It happened too suddenly. A heart attack.'

Her heart went out to him. She could sense his pain, even under the dispassionate mask he was sheltering behind. It gave her a peculiar quiver, to realise that she could still feel for him at all, let alone sense the pain he hid so well.

So Tom and his father had never seen each other again…had never had a chance to make their peace with each other. How sad, she thought. Poor Tom. No wonder he's hurting.

'And your stepmother?' she asked tentatively. 'How is she?'

Tom shrugged. 'Meryl's probably already on her third husband. I haven't seen her since the funeral.' He glanced up, his expression changing. She could virtually see him shaking off the past. Shaking off any betraying emotion. 'Did you get through to Charlie?' he asked, switching the subject.

'Yes, I did,' she said, and knitted her brow. 'At least I got through to Aunt Edith. I couldn't speak to my father because he has laryngitis now. He's lost his voice completely.'

'Poor old Charlie.' Tom's tanned face crinkled, his lips easing into the familiar lopsided grin. 'He's having a rough trot.'

Something in his voice made her look at him more closely. He wasn't taking it very seriously, she thought.

Her frown deepened. A nasty suspicion was growing.

No…it wasn't possible. It couldn't be. Her father wouldn't *pretend* to be sick, would he, simply to get out of the trip to Kakadu, forcing her to go with—

Tom Scanlon!

She reached shakily for her glass. Charlie had already been devious once, failing to warn her about Tom. But would he be *this* devious?

When her entrée arrived, she leaned over her plate as if to examine the marinated pieces of crocodile in her tossed avocado and lettuce salad, but her mind was hurtling on at a furious rate. It was no use asking Tom. If her suspicion was true, and Tom was a party to it, he would hardly admit it. He'd bluff it out somehow.

If it was true.

It couldn't be! Charlie wouldn't be so cruel to his only daughter! To plan this whole outrageous scenario deliberately, callously throwing her to the wolves—the wolves in this instance being her ex-fiancé, not Kakadu's wild dingoes—and blithely disregarding the consequences.

It was bad enough knowing her father had appealed to Tom Scanlon for help when he'd fallen ill—assuming he *had* fallen ill. She could have understood Charlie wanting to find someone they knew—a *friend*—to look after his daughter at Kakadu.

But why choose her ex-fiancé, of all people? A man who'd hurt and humiliated her? A man she clearly despised!

Why would her father want to throw them back together?

It would be no good asking Charlie. He'd simply say there'd been no one else to ask at such short notice, and argue that if he'd told her about Tom in advance, she wouldn't have gone. And she'd *had* to go, Charlie would have defended himself, or her career would have suffered. Asking Tom, he would insist, had been his only solution.

And the amazing, infuriating, unbelievable thing was that Tom had actually agreed.

Had he agreed readily, she brooded, or had her father been forced to do some fast talking, some subtle arm-twisting? Or had he called Tom simply to ask if he knew of anybody who could look after his daughter for a couple of weeks, only to have Tom jump at the chance, seeing it as a perfect way to worm himself back into her life?

She frowned, barely noticing the taste of her sauteed crocodile or its sweet soy and honey dressing, as an even more outrageous thought struck her. *Had this whole painful charade been Tom's idea in the first place?* Had he suggested to her father, when he had Charlie alone in their art gallery yesterday, that Charlie feign illness to clear the way for *him?*

She nearly choked on a piece of crocodile meat. Snatching up her napkin, she coughed into its folds, dabbing furiously at her lips. The wine must be going to her head. It was too far-fetched for words! She'd *seen* her father, for heaven's sake, and he'd been really sick, hardly able to raise his head. Charlie couldn't be that good an actor. *Could* he?

She jerked a furious shoulder. If Tom Scanlon had put her father up to this…

She glared across the table at him.

'You don't like your crocodile?' Tom asked mildly, his face as bland as his tone. His blue eyes were gently inquiring.

'It's fine.' *I just don't like what I'm thinking.* But to actually come out and accuse Tom…to say that she didn't believe that her father was sick at all…

It would sound too callous and hysterical for words!

If she was wrong, she'd be making a complete fool of herself.

Besides, it would be crazy to risk starting a fight here in the restaurant, when she was so determined to keep her cool and stay aloof.

No… She would wait until she'd had a chance to speak to her father. She would ask him, not Tom Scanlon. She would grill Charlie until he told her the truth. And once she knew, then she would decide how to deal with it.

'We'd better start planning our program for tomorrow,' she said querulously. 'I want to go to Nourlangie Rock first up. Early…before the tourist buses start arriving. You've been there before yourself?'

'A number of times.' Tom sat back in his chair and proceeded to tell her about the massive rock, originally part of the Arnhem Land escarpment, and about the ancient Aboriginal rock paintings covering its walls, attracting sightseers from all over the world.

Natasha kept the conversation on the same safe path until they'd finished their main course. Then, declining dessert—enticing as the dessert menu looked—she burrowed into her purse. She'd noted the prices of everything she'd ordered, including her glass of wine.

She put some notes on the table. 'That should cover my share, plus a tip. Would you take care of it?' she asked Tom, rising as she spoke. 'I need to go to bed. I'm bushed.' She paused only to add, 'I'll meet you in the foyer at seven.' She would grab some orange juice and fresh fruit before then for breakfast.

As she swung away, Tom's deep voice wafted after her. 'Peaceful dreams, Natasha.'

She faltered, a quiver rippling down her spine.

Peaceful dreams? With Tom Scanlon sleeping in the room next door? Knowing he'd be sleeping even closer in the nights to come? She hadn't had a peaceful dream since he'd come back into her life!

Who are you kidding, Natasha Beale? You haven't had a peaceful dream since Tom Scanlon walked out of your life eighteen months ago!

CHAPTER FIVE

A LOW mist hung over the bush as they drove to Nourlangie Rock. The eucalypts rang with bird sounds, from the sweetest melodies to the harshest, most penetrating squawks. Natasha sat perkily in the passenger seat, her spirits revived after a surprisingly good night's sleep. Even the sight of Tom this morning hadn't dampened her good humour.

Today she was going to start work—and concentrate only on that. She had her camera, sketchbook and painting gear ready: paintbrushes, a travel set of watercolour paints, and a folder of watercolour paper. She could hardly wait.

If she could keep her mind fixed on the fascinating sights around her and the wonderful landscapes she was going to paint, and if she refused to think about Tom, she would come through this ordeal. She had to stop seeing him as her ex-fiancé. She had to stop marvelling at his sexy new look.

She jolted upright. *There you go again, you fool!*

She blinked him away, then abruptly sat forward. 'There's a kangaroo!' she cried, glad that something had relieved the monotony of the mist-shrouded bush on either side, allowing her to snap her thoughts away from Tom Scanlon.

'It's a wallaroo—a hill kangaroo.' Tom slowed the vehicle as the animal hopped into the shelter of the trees. 'You'll see a lot of them in the dry, rocky country—which we're coming into now. Rock wallabies too.'

The new rugged terrain kept the conversation going, and her mind occupied, until Tom found a shady parking spot in the car park below Nourlangie Rock. The majestic sandstone walls of the massive Rock rose above them, its rugged outline stark against the clear blue sky.

'Don't forget your water bottle,' Tom reminded her as she gathered up her camera, paints and sketchbook. 'Or your hat.' His gaze swept approvingly over her loose jungle green shirt, baggy shorts and walking boots. 'And you might need some insect repellent for any exposed skin.' His eyes were on her legs, she noticed, feeling her skin prickle in response. 'The flies can be annoying round here.'

She dutifully did as he suggested, then pulled a peaked cap over her blond ponytail to shade her face, which she'd already plastered with a moisturising sunscreen.

'I'd like to get the feel of the Rock first,' she said, keeping her tone brisk and businesslike. 'I'm going to climb up and see the rock paintings and then take the longer track up to the lookout. I'll take some close-up photographs, then come back down and take some more shots from a distance, and do some sketching and painting.' Most of her paintings for the exhibition would be completed back home, using her sketches, photographs, notes, and daubs of watercolour for accuracy.

She marched off, half hoping Tom would decide to stay close to his four-wheel-drive in the shade—or else do some exploring of his own.

No such luck. He followed her every step of the way. Or *led* her, rather. He seemed to know Nourlangie Rock like the back of his hand, and was able to relate the story of every rock painting as if he'd been born to the place.

Which he hadn't, of course. He'd been born and raised on the northern coast of New South Wales, in the industrial town of Newcastle. But he'd always yearned for the bush and the open spaces, and as soon as he'd finished his studies he'd left Newcastle to work on a Queensland cattle station—the start of his adventurous outback life.

She had no idea what kind of work Tom had taken on in Sydney after he'd broken off their engagement, and she didn't intend to ask. But he must have tired quickly of city life, if he'd been running adventure safaris in the Top End for the past year.

Her eyebrows slanted in a frown. No doubt he'd been running away from his Sydney girlfriend as much as from the city. Running away from commitment. Again. *It didn't work out,* he'd told her airily, without the faintest sign of any pain or regret or compassion for the woman he'd left behind. He'd tried a new relationship and it had failed. Too bad. Time to move on.

She clenched her teeth as she raised her camera for one final shot from her present position, back at the base of the Rock.

It didn't work out… Such a handy little phrase. Such an easy way out. Had he used that same phrase to his girlfriend eighteen months ago, to explain away the fiancée he'd ditched? *Natasha's out of my life now… It didn't work out.*

If he'd even bothered to mention her at all!

'Ouch!' She almost leapt into the air. She'd taken a step back without thinking, without looking, and her bare leg had come in contact with a prickly flowering shrub. She reached down to rub the irritated patch of skin.

She heard a laugh and her head jerked round. Tom was standing a few feet away, his hands on his hips, *laughing*. Laughing at her discomfort!

'It's not funny,' she snarled. 'It hurts.'

'It would have hurt a lot more if you'd trodden on a death adder. Snakes love hiding in shrubs. You're supposed to look where you're treading out here in the bush.'

She snapped her mouth shut. Insensitive monster, she thought. Even if he's right, damn him!

'Want some soothing ointment on it?' Tom

asked, belatedly showing some sympathy. 'There's some in the car.'

'I'll survive,' she muttered.

'We should go back anyway, and grab something to eat.'

Tom had asked the hotel to make up some sandwiches. He'd also magically produced muesli bars and apples to munch during the morning, and kept her water bottle topped up. The man, she had to concede, was amazingly efficient.

She chopped off the thought, incensed that she was thinking about him again.

The evening approached only too quickly. They'd spent the whole day at Nourlangie Rock, until she'd absorbed every nook and cranny and imprinted it all into her memory. She'd done a little painting and taken lots of photographs, and filled her notebook with sketches. They'd stayed at the Rock until the sun began to sink, giving the towering sandstone walls a pinkish hue, before turning them to a vivid burnt sienna. Then as the earth darkened and the Rock took on a bluish tinge, they drove off along one of the dirt tracks, heading for the camping ground where they planned to spend the night.

Tom drove carefully, aware that dusk was the most dangerous time on the road, with kangaroos and wallabies likely to jump out from nowhere. They saw a number hopping through the bush, but only one small wallaby crossed their path, at a safe enough distance to avoid.

Natasha had other worries. By the time they reached the camp site, her heart was almost leaping out of her chest at the thought of the night ahead.

They were the first campers to arrive. Would there be any others? she wondered with a nervous glance round. This was an out-of-the-way camp site. They were off the usual tourist track now, deep in the rugged stone country. She'd wanted to come here because it was within walking distance—a long bush walk—of an interesting gorge and rainforest area that she was keen to paint.

There was a small billabong adjacent to the campsite, the water glassy in the fading light. Tall spindly eucalyptus trees cast ghostly shadows, their branches ringing with trills and chirrups and warbles. A kookaburra cackled, the harsh sound piercing the sultry evening air.

As they unloaded the four-wheel-drive, Natasha drew in a deep breath and let it out in a sigh. At one time she might have seen this as a romantic spot—an idyllic place to spend a night. A night with one's lover.

Only she didn't have a lover...

How ironic that the man she'd once loved should be here with her now...a dangerous, disturbing, nerve-racking presence.

A shiver of apprehension brushed down her

spine—just as something large, black and sinister-looking soared overhead.

She ducked instinctively. 'Wh-what was that?'

'A vampire,' Tom said, licking his lips. 'Better known as a flying fox.' He grinned. 'They come out at night looking for fruit and blossom.'

He'd removed his hat and was running his fingers through his hair, as if to let some air through it. Watching him, Natasha recalled, in an unwanted memory flash, how she'd often run her own fingers through the rumpled softness of his hair. Loving the feel of it. Even now they itched to—

She cut off the impulse in shocked horror. Disgusted with herself, she wrenched her gaze away.

'Like a cold drink first up?' Tom was burrowing into his portable fridge.

'Yes, please.' She needed it! Her mouth suddenly felt bone dry.

'Like a Diet Pepsi for a change?' They'd been drinking water all day. Litres of it.

'Thanks.' *Diet* Pepsi, she noted. 'That sounds good.' Anything cold and fizzy sounded good.

There were no facilities at the campground, other than primitive pit toilets. There were no showers, no gas barbecues, and no water supply—other than the billabong. They had to gather wood to start a fire in the simple fireplace provided.

'You'll find a couple of buckets in the car,' Tom

told her as the fire sprang to life under his expert fingers. 'If you fill them from the billabong, you could have a wash and get the dust and grime off. Use the other bucket to rinse off.'

She paused, biting her lip. Wash in a bucket of water when there was a cool fresh billabong luring her like a siren? She looked longingly at the invitingly tranquil water, silvery under the rising moon.

'What if I just dunk myself in the billabong?' she suggested, and flushed as Tom's eyebrows rose in the flickering firelight. 'With my clothes on, I mean,' she hastened to add. As if she'd strip off and jump in *naked* with Tom Scanlon looking on! 'I could wash myself and my clothes at the same time.' After the heat and dust of the day it sounded heavenly. 'I'll just fetch some soap and a—'

'Forget it.' His voice was sharp. 'We don't wash or even clean our teeth in the billabongs—it could harm the fish and pollute someone's drinking water. The crocodiles mightn't like it either,' he added warningly. 'Then again…' His eyes mocked her, a predatory glint discernible in the soft moonlight. 'Maybe they might—if they haven't had their dinner yet.'

'Crocodiles?' Startled, she raked her gaze over the glassy surface of the water. There wasn't a ripple. 'You're just trying to scare me.'

'Not at all. In Kakadu, it's wise to assume that any body of water could be harbouring a crocodile.

Once the floodwaters go down, crocs can end up in any of the pools and creeks left behind.'

She shuddered. 'But wouldn't we see some sign of them? A pair of eyes, the top of a head, some movement in the water? Nothing has surfaced since we arrived here.'

'Crocodiles can stay underwater for an hour or more.' Tom grinned as wide eyes flew to his. 'I'd better come with you when you fill the buckets— just to be on the safe side. Your father would never forgive me if I let a croc grab you.'

She eyed him uncertainly, not sure if he was serious or not about lurking crocodiles. But she let him come with her to the edge of the billabong, and could feel his watchful, protective presence as she lowered the first bucket into the water. As she raised it she felt his hand gripping the handle, easing it from her.

'Here, let me. It's heavy.'

It wasn't too heavy for her, but she didn't protest as she filled the second bucket, letting him carry both of them to a sheltered spot under the trees, well away from the bank. Best not to make a fuss about anything in this remote, moon-drenched hideaway, she decided. The atmosphere was highly charged enough already. She trembled as Tom put the buckets down and turned to face her.

'Okay, start washing,' he said, 'while I get dinner underway.' He'd already fetched various foodstuffs from the four-wheel-drive, and she'd brought what she needed to freshen herself up—and some mosquito repellent, which Tom had warned was vital at night, especially near water.

She set to work, in the relative privacy of some small leafy gum trees and native shrubs. Since she hadn't dunked herself, fully clothed, in the billabong, she had no soaked clothes to dry or change out of, so she kept on the same shirt and shorts. She could change later in her tent—if she changed at all. As she was dabbing her face with a towel, her nose began to twitch at the delicious aromas drifting across the campsite.

Onions. There was nothing quite like the smell of cooking onions!

She drifted closer to the fire, not sure if it was the food that was drawing her like a moth to a flame, or the welcoming safety of the fire. One thing she knew—it wasn't Tom Scanlon luring her there. She'd be running in the opposite direction if she'd had any choice!

'Oh!' She jumped back as something scurried underfoot. She saw a small lizard vanish into the bushes.

'Something wrong?' Tom turned sharply.

She gave an embarrassed laugh. She must try to be more prepared for the unexpected, less quick to react like a startled, city-bred adolescent!

'Just a lizard.' What other creatures, she paused

to wonder, would start emerging from the bush,
now that it was dark? Snakes? Rock pythons? Giant
goannas? Big crawly spiders?

She tried not to think about it!

She almost scurried the rest of the way to the fire.
'Mm…that smells great.' Her nostrils were twitching again, her mouth watering at the sight of the
two huge steaks sizzling on Tom's portable hotplate, with tomatoes, onions and red peppers brown-
ing alongside. Foil-wrapped potatoes were baking
in the fire. A blackened saucepan was simmering at
the rear of the hotplate.

Peas and carrots, she guessed, noting the label on
an empty can lying beside the fire.

A veritable feast! She'd never known Tom to
cook before—to go to the trouble of cooking. It had
always been easier and quicker to grab a takeaway
pizza or to buy a bag of French fries.

'Where did you get the steaks?' she asked in
amazement. Here they were, in the back blocks of
Kakadu Park, having spent a full day out in the
searing heat, and he'd managed to produce fresh
meat! Although the four-wheel-drive had been in
the shade of the trees for most of the day, the heat
inside would still have been intense.

'I bought them at Jabaru this morning, and
they've been in the portable frig all day.' Tom's
dancing eyes met hers. 'Hungry?'

'Ravenous.' She swallowed, wishing he wouldn't look at her like that. It reminded her too much of the Tom he'd used to be.

'Then fetch the plates. It's ready.'

CHAPTER SIX

THEY sat round the fire to eat. Besides throwing out warmth, the bright glow of the flames gave Natasha a comforting sense of safety and security. Other dangerous creatures could be roaming about in the dark. Dingoes…feral pigs…wild buffalo…

But nothing disturbed the peaceful tranquillity— other than the sound of crickets, frogs, owls, and some mysterious twitterings from the bush. And the incessant buzz of mosquitoes! They'd had to smother their exposed hands, necks, faces and ankles with repellent. By now the full moon was high in the sky, flooding the camp site with its pearly light. A myriad stars filled the soft black sky.

Natasha should have been feeling tranquil too, but she wasn't. She was feeling more jumpy by the minute—and it had nothing to do with wild creatures lurking in the bush. It was the human creature sitting opposite her she feared the most—even though she'd denied it vehemently last night when he'd taunted her about being afraid.

She was afraid. She was afraid of what he could still do to her, with just a look, a touch, a smile. Heaven knew what effect he might have on her if he ever decided to grab her in his arms and *kiss* her!

She recoiled at the unbidden thought. Horrified at the direction her mind was going, she scrambled to her feet, giving an exaggerated yawn as she straightened.

'It's been a long day. Time to turn in,' she mumbled. 'If you'll find the tent for me, Tom, I'll put it up.'

He lifted a teasing eyebrow as he stood up. 'You feel you need a tent, on a glorious night like this? You don't want to sleep out under the stars, and feel at one with nature?' His blue eyes glinted a challenge.

'And be eaten alive by mosquitoes?' she shot back, her heart jumping erratically at the thought of lying out under the stars with her rakish ex-fiancé. 'No, thanks.'

'You could have a mosquito net over you.'

'I'll feel safer in a tent.'

His brow shot up again, a crooked half-smile on his lips. 'Safer from me, do you mean?'

'Of course not,' she denied hotly, trying to believe it. 'From—from wild animals. What if one of those ferocious wild pigs decided to charge through our camp site?' She'd already spied a couple of rock wallabies and a kangaroo, hopping silently to the edge of the billabong to drink.

'I could set up trip wires, if it would make you feel safer. But I'm sure you'll be perfectly safe here at the camp site. I'll keep the fire going.'

A deep indrawn breath swelled her chest. 'Tom, if you won't fetch the tent, I'll go and find it myself.'

'Okay, okay, if you insist. But you'll be missing out on a sublime experience.'

She gave a snort. A sublime experience? Lying out in the open with her ex-fiancé sprawled out beside her? She wouldn't be able to relax for a second! And after her long, tiring day she badly wanted to relax. She needed her sleep! Tomorrow was going to be an even longer, tougher day than today. They had a long hard bush walk ahead of them to the gorge, and another long hard trek back here to the camp site.

If they had time to come all the way back in the one day. When her father had applied for the permits they'd need, he'd requested one that would allow them to camp out overnight on this particular bush walk—if it became necessary.

She would just have to make sure that it didn't! Because if she and Tom failed to make it back here by nightfall, she would have to sleep out under the stars *then*. She certainly wasn't lugging a tent all the way to the gorge and back! They would already have their bedding and supplies, and they'd have cameras and water bottles slung round their necks.

Her breath was quickening, her heartbeat racing, doing an erratic dance. Why hadn't she cut this out-of-the-way gorge from her schedule, the minute

Tom Scanlon appeared on the scene? Why hadn't she stuck to the familiar tourist haunts, where there were civilised facilities at hand and always other people around?

Because you're a professional, that's why, she reproached herself. You're here in the Park to find the best possible settings to paint—to show Kakadu at its wildest and best—and this hard-to-reach gorge is definitely one of the best!

She heard Tom's voice at her elbow. 'Want some help?' He had the tent in his arms.

'I can manage.' Did he think she'd never camped out before, never pitched a tent before?

'If you say so. While you're doing that, I'll gather up the rubbish and clean up. Mustn't leave food scraps lying around to attract the dingoes…or any other wild animals, for that matter.' In the glow of the camp fire, his eyes seemed to burn like one of the wild animals he was warning her about!

'I won't leave anything lying about,' she bit back, her nerves unravelling a bit more.

'And don't pitch your tent anywhere near the water's edge,' he warned. 'Remember the crocs. To say nothing of the mozzies.'

'I'm not that silly.' She stifled a shiver. There were more predators threatening her here at this camp site, it seemed, than any other camping ground she'd ever known.

And the most dangerous predator of all was the one who was throwing out all the warnings!

She pitched her tent at a safe distance from the peaceful-looking billabong—and as far from the fire, where Tom would undoubtedly bunk down, as she could.

She fumbled once or twice as she put the tent up, but she finally managed without having to suffer the indignity of having to call on Tom for help.

It was a two-man tent—quite roomy, but hardly big enough for two grown adults to comfortably share—thank heaven. It was perfect, though, for one. The floor would protect her from any creepy crawlies, and the zip-up door would protect her from flying insects, wandering animals, and the dreaded mosquitoes.

And also protect her from her smouldering-eyed travel companion!

Tom was unrolling his sleeping bag, she noticed, under a clump of thin saplings, not far from the fire. While he was busily occupied, she slipped across to the pit toilet, hoping it was free of spiders.

As she was making her way back to her tent, Tom ambled across to meet her—a dark hulking figure in the silvery moonlight.

'Turning in now?' he asked pleasantly.

'That's the general idea.' Her tone was edgy.

'Ah...well, good night, Natasha.' He paused. He was standing very close, his great shoulders a shadowy silhouette against the brightness of the moon. 'Do I get a goodnight kiss?' he asked hopefully.

Her heart leapt in panic. She took a step back. He wouldn't dare try… 'You've got to be joking.' The rebuff was withering, but she felt as if her breath had clogged in her throat.

'Not even a friendly thank-you kiss? For cooking you a scrumptious dinner?'

She eyed him warily. His lips were stretched in an easy grin. There was a playful twinkle in his eye. His stance was relaxed, his hands resting loosely on his hips. He didn't look as if he were about to pounce, and attempt to ravish her against her will. He didn't look the least bit menacing.

And yet she felt scared to death!

'Thank you for a scrumptious dinner,' she jerked out through dry lips, attempting a facetious note.

'Our dinner tomorrow night won't be anywhere near as lavish,' he warned, a wheedling note in his voice. 'Probably just freeze-dried veggies and canned tuna.' He cocked his head at her. 'I just thought—'

'Well, don't!' She tried to control her breathing, which was going haywire, along with her heartbeat. Was this just a playful try-on, to see how she'd react?

Or was he testing her, to see if he could make her weaken, and reveal that she did still have some feeling for him?

I'll show you how I feel, Tom Scanlon! She gulped. If she didn't, she'd be lost.

She tossed back her head and laughed. A brief, scathing laugh. 'Good try, Tom, but it won't work.' She marvelled that she could sound so cool and in control, when her heart was pumping overtime, her lips tingling at the thought of his mouth crushing hers, her body trembling with the urge to melt against him.

If he only knew how dangerously close she *was* to weakening!

She swallowed—and thought of the woman he'd preferred to *her*.

It was all she needed. She screwed up her nose in distaste. 'I think I'd be sick if you tried to kiss me, Tom Scanlon!' That should dampen his ardour! She jutted her chin to press home her point. 'You seem to be forgetting you're just my tour guide— and only for the duration of this trip. Then it's good-bye. For good.' She trembled at the finality of it. But she meant it! 'Understood?'

She didn't wait around for an answer. But as she swung away, Tom caught up in one long swift stride.

'Tash, wait—' He caught her arm.

She wheeled round, her stomach knotting. Did he know what he was doing to her? Did he know how long it had taken her to crawl out of the pit of despair she'd floundered in after he'd left her? And it seemed she wasn't over him yet! She still despised him for what he'd done to her, and yet—

She bit back a moan. Incredibly, she still longed for him too.

But she mustn't! She'd be mad to let him sweep her off her feet a second time. Even if he'd changed, even if he regretted what he'd done, how would she ever be able to trust him again?

To cover her rising panic, she summoned a burst of white-hot fury. 'Don't call me that!' Blazing eyes flayed him. 'And let go of me!'

He dropped his hand. As her fiery gaze met the blue glitter of his, she wavered, frowning up at him. The playful glint had died from his eyes. He suddenly looked unnervingly serious, his brow drawn, his jaw tight, as if he had some weighty problem on his mind.

'What's wrong?' she demanded shakily. 'Did you forget to warn me that a grizzly bear is loose in the park?'

His eyes gleamed in the wash of the moonlight. 'Not quite.' A brief smile flickered. 'It's just—' He took one look at her mutinous face and heaved a sigh. 'Never mind. You're tired and it's getting late.' He stood aside to let her pass. 'Good night, Natasha.'

'Good night, Tom,' she said stiffly, and scurried past him, into the sanctuary of her tent, refusing to even think about what he'd been going to say. Once inside, she zipped the door securely, and with a tremulous sigh, part relief, part weariness, she wriggled, fully clothed, into her sleeping bag.

But sleep didn't come straightaway, even though her sleeping bag was comfortable enough, and the zipped-up door of her tent protected her from the mosquitoes she could hear buzzing about outside.

She could hear every sound—every crackle, every rustle, every twitter. Eventually a new sound reached her ears. A soft melodic sound. A haunting, gently soothing sound.

A sound that brought back a rush of romantic, nostalgic memories.

It was Tom, playing his mouth organ!

She lay still, barely breathing. The last time she'd heard him playing it was on a outback trip they'd taken together, when she'd flown with him on one of his helicopter flights to visit a Queensland cattle station. They'd sat around a glowing camp fire in the evening and he'd played these very same tunes.

She felt a warm tear trickle down her cheek, tasting its salty moistness as it ran into her mouth. They'd been so happy together…had felt so fulfilled and complete together—or so she'd thought. What had Tom found lacking in her that had made him walk out on her, straight into the arms of another woman? What had he been seeking that he hadn't found in *her?*

He obviously hadn't found it in his new girlfriend

either! He'd dismissed his new love as easily as he had his fiancée of two weeks.

Maybe *he* was the one who was lacking. Lacking staying ability.

But he'd come back!

Why had he come back? Because he'd found that the grass on the other side of the fence hadn't been any greener after all?

Maybe her father was right. Maybe Tom had simply felt trapped, wary at the idea of marriage, and he'd panicked. Maybe he'd just needed some breathing space for a while, to get his head back together, and had taken up with another woman on the rebound—a woman who'd meant nothing to him, despite what he'd said at the time...*I didn't mean it to happen, Tash...it hit me like a bolt out of the blue.*

It must have been pure lust...a scorching, too-hot-to-last affair...nothing to do with deep, lasting feelings. If Tom even knew the meaning of the word 'lasting.'

She shivered. Did he honestly believe she might give him another chance?

Was that why he was playing those familiar, haunting melodies? To remind her of their romantic evenings alone together? To lull her—*seduce* her—into lowering her defenses?

If Tom Scanlon was serenading her as a first step

to a full-scale seduction, hoping that she'd forgive him and take him back…

She blinked furiously, dashing away her tears. *It's too late, Tom.* She closed her ears to the poignant sounds drifting from the camp fire. *I could never take you back…I'd never be able to trust you again!*

She pulled the sleeping bag over her head and began to hum, *I'm going to wash that man right out of my head*, over and over, furiously concentrating on that one song and nothing else.

She kept on humming until she fell asleep.

She still had tears on her cheeks.

CHAPTER SEVEN

'HEY, sweetheart…if you keep up this pace you'll be burnt out before we reach the gorge.'

Natasha threw a brief glance over her shoulder, but didn't slow down. 'Are you having trouble keeping up?' she taunted, ignoring the drawled endearment. 'Sweetheart' meant nothing—and it was preferable to 'Tash.' 'Tash' was far too close, too intimate. He had no right to be so intimate. Not any more.

'I'm being sensible. You're not,' he growled. 'It's time you stopped for a breather. And a drink. I don't want to have to carry you if you collapse.'

'I won't collapse,' she shot back. 'And I've been taking sips of my drink.' She wasn't that silly. But she felt a flush rising, knowing she should have been taking more sips. Longer sips. Only she hadn't wanted anything to slow her down!

'Well, stop now and have a proper drink.' Tom's tone was implacable. 'I know you're keen to see this gorge, Natasha, but when you're out bushwalking, especially in heat like this, you have to be careful.'

'Okay, okay,' she said fractiously, and paused

obediently, secretly glad to catch her breath. He was right. In this humid heat, with a heavy backpack, a camera and a water bottle slung round her neck, and a rough bush track underfoot, she was going to collapse if she didn't take it a bit easier.

She'd made the right decision not to bring her bulky watercolour folder and set of paints today! She'd only brought her sketchbook and camera.

As she took a long swig from her water bottle, Tom produced a muesli bar from his pack and took a hefty bite. 'You eat something too,' he advised between mouthfuls. 'It'll keep your strength up.'

'I'm fine. I'm not—'

'Eat something! We're not moving till you do.'

She glowered at him. 'I never realised what a bully you were,' she grumbled, then wished she hadn't reminded him that they'd shared a past once. She opened her bag and pulled out a banana. After she'd taken a couple of bites she said, 'Okay, let's go.' She could eat the rest on the way. 'I promise I won't walk too fast for you.'

Tom sighed. 'It's not me I'm worried about.' He frowned as she swung away. 'You'll have plenty of time to spend at this gorge we're going to, so what's your hurry?'

Without glancing round, she admitted carelessly, 'I'd like to be back at the camping ground before dark.'

Tom gave a snort as he caught up with her. 'Not a hope! Even if you ran all the way there and back and didn't take a single photograph of the gorge or the rainforest you're so keen to see. We'll have to camp out overnight on the way back. We'll have no choice. I thought you realised that. You applied for a permit.'

Feeling her cheeks burning, she averted her face. 'I just thought, if we put a spurt on…' She sighed, seeing her arguments slipping away. 'It's just that…' She gulped. 'I'd rather sleep in a tent than out among the mosquitoes,' she mumbled—only she wasn't thinking of mosquitoes.

'I brought the repellent. And you're well covered up.' He'd made her wear a long-sleeved shirt today to protect her from the sun, and jeans to protect her from the sharp grasses—and possible snakes.

She twitched a careless shoulder, not wanting him to think that camping out overnight seriously bothered her. Not wanting him to think that *he* was the reason she wanted to avoid sleeping out under the stars. As if he didn't know.

She could sense his eyes on her, amused eyes, mocking her. He was right, she had to grudgingly admit. They hadn't a hope of making it back to the camp site tonight, so she might as well stop rushing through the bush like a wild boar and start noticing what she'd come to see.

Before long she had no choice but to start noticing. The bushland gave way to rugged rock faces and huge boulders, and the going became steeper, harder underfoot and more difficult, needing all her concentration. She paused a few times to take photographs—a close-up of a rock wallaby sunning itself on the rocks...a red-winged parrot sitting on a branch...a turkey bush, seemingly growing out of sheer rock.

Eventually, as they descended into the cool haven of the sheltered gorge, she forgot she'd ever been in a hurry. Lush ferns, vines and rainforest trees grew among the ancient rocks. There were cool, hidden places everywhere—in sharp contrast to the dry exposed surfaces of the arid, rocky Escarpment.

'It's beautiful,' Natasha whispered, and tensed as her hand brushed Tom's in the confined space. Nerves bristling, she bit back an involuntary gasp as she came face to face with a giant cave gecko, lying on the cool rocks.

Instinctively, she raised her camera and managed to take a shot before the scaly lizard retreated to safety. For an hour or more she took photographs of the magical place, moving around to capture the best angles. She took more snaps out in the open among the giant boulders and the rich tangled ferns and tropical palms of the rainforest, where Tom had found a shady spot to have lunch.

A small waterfall tinkled in cascading steps down the rocky hillside, through thickets of grevillea and wattle, to a crystal clear pool below.

Paradise!

She didn't linger over their simple snack. She pulled out her sketchbook and let her pencil fly. Tom didn't disturb her by talking. He seemed content to rest in the shade. And just watch her.

She was certain he was watching her, even though each time she glanced his way he appeared to have his eyes closed, shaded by his broad-brimmed hat. She tried not to let his presence wreck her concentration—though her hand, to her annoyance, had become unusually shaky, and she had to pause every now and then to steady it.

Before following a different bush track back— one that would eventually join up with their original track—they refilled their water bottles in the fresh forest pool. Natasha stopped often to take photographs or to make notes or sketches—there was no hurry now. The sun was already low in the sky and the shadows were lengthening.

She gulped. Hard. Night would be here soon. All too soon.

They glimpsed more wallabies and wallaroos as the heat of the day passed its peak. Lizards scuttled underfoot. Natasha was marching ahead of Tom, with her hand ready on her camera. She'd already gone through several films, and would soon be needing another. She glanced down to check how much film she had left in the camera.

And stiffened as she felt Tom's hand clasp her shoulder.

As she snapped her head up, ready to shake it off, his grip tightened, his fingers digging into her flesh.

She wheeled round to give him a piece of her mind. But as her lips parted they were smothered by his—fiercely smothered, his mouth effectively sealing hers. A strong hand clamped over her peaked cap, preventing her from drawing back. His other arm held her in a steel-like grip that effectively stopped any movement at all.

Outraged as she was, she felt a hot, tingling weakness sweep through her. For a second she felt too mesmerised, too weak-kneed to protest. She'd loved these lips once. They'd always had this heady, melting effect on her. It amazed her—dismayed her—that they still did.

It was no use struggling. It would be futile anyway, futile and humiliating. His grip was like a vice. She knew he wouldn't hurt her—beyond the indignity of this outrageous kiss. She sensed instinctively that she had nothing to fear from Tom—even though she was going to give him a sharp tongue-lashing the second he set her free!

But when he did lift his mouth, just a fraction, it was to hiss, 'Don't make a sound. Don't move. Don't even breathe.' His gaze caught hers, compelling her with its force—forbidding her to scream. 'Take a glance over to your left.'

Heart thumping, she followed his look. Tom's hand whipped over her lips as she sucked in her breath. She glowered, to let him know she had no intention of screaming—though she felt like it. Only metres ahead, blocking the track, stood a hefty, ferocious-looking water buffalo!

Despite her shaking knees, and a powerful urge to run for her life, she felt an artist's sense of awe, her fingers itching to raise her camera or grab her sketchbook. She'd never expected to see a wild buffalo—especially so close. They were so destructive they'd been largely wiped out and were rarely seen in the wild any more.

'Don't even think it,' Tom muttered, as if reading her mind. 'If he spots us he could take an acute dislike to us. Feral buffaloes,' he warned, 'are dangerous. They can cause nasty injuries.'

Natasha tilted her chin—even as a shiver ran down her spine. She was fully aware that wild buffaloes were dangerous. She'd read the warnings in her guide book. *Keep at a safe distance—do not approach.* But she'd never expected to meet one, almost nose to nose!

'Just stand still,' Tom commanded in a whisper. 'If he doesn't go away in the next few minutes we'll back up a bit—slowly—and make a wide detour.'

She dutifully kept still, hardly breathing, her camera and sketchbook forgotten. She wasn't about to take any stupid risks. A charging buffalo was the last thing she needed!

A kangaroo hopped across the track ahead, and she hissed in her breath, leaning back against Tom for a startled second. A flock of sulphur-crested cockatoos fluttered squawking into the air. Disturbed, the big buffalo finally lumbered away from the track, heading deeper into the bush.

'Come on, it's okay now...' Releasing her, Tom ushered her forward. 'We'd better get a move on. I want to find a suitable spot to camp overnight before it gets dark.'

The prospect of camping out overnight with Tom suddenly held new terrors. 'Wh-what if the buffalo comes back while we're sleeping?' she asked tremulously, keeping a wary eye on the surrounding bush as she hurried along beside him, careful not to lag behind. The evenings in Kakadu Park might be beautiful, with the twinkling stars and the silvery moon and the fascinating sounds of the bush, but they could be hair-raising too.

'It won't. It'll be wallowing in some marsh somewhere by now, miles away. Nothing's going to

harm you, Nat. Wild animals don't seek out trouble.
And we'll have a fire. I'll keep it going all night.'

She felt something waver inside her. *Nat*, he was
calling her now. Had he given up on 'Tash' at last?
Stopped thinking of her as Tash? Stopped trying to
get closer? It wasn't as if he'd really kissed her a
moment ago. That hadn't been a genuine kiss. He'd
just wanted to shut her up. In a hurry.

Well, I hope he *has* decided to back off, she
thought with a toss of her head. He's finally getting
the message.

There was something mellowing—romantic even—
about sitting around a camp fire in the balmy air of
evening, with the pungent tang of the bush all
around and the full moon on the rise and the stars
a sparkling curtain above.

Very mellowing.

And Natasha was feeling distinctly mellow.
They'd set up camp in a small clearing between a
mound of rocks and a forest of spindly eucalypts
and leafy billygoat plums. Sitting on their folded
sleeping bags, they were enjoying a simply prepared
meal out of a can, heated over the camp fire—with
some rum that Tom had poured from a small flask
into two tumblers.

'I keep it for medicinal purposes,' had been his
drawled comment.

She took another sip and felt it coursing down her throat in a fiery path, then spreading its heat through her veins. 'I think it's going to my head,' she murmured. 'I feel very relaxed.'

'Well, you could do with some relaxing, after that scare.' Tom's eyes were tender rather than mocking. For a fuzzy second she thought he was talking about his kiss earlier—she certainly needed something to relax her after a scare like that!—until she realised he was referring to the wild buffalo.

The softness in his eyes sobered her as nothing else could. He shouldn't be looking at her like that…and she shouldn't be getting tipsy—not while she was in Tom Scanlon's lethal company.

With a jut of her jaw, she growled accusingly, 'You didn't have to *kiss* me to keep me quiet!'

Tom grinned, showing no repentance at all. 'You were about to yell at me. I had to stop you. Our friend the buffalo was too close for comfort, if you recall. A sudden shout could have provoked him into charging.'

She twitched, preferring not to think about it. 'Well, if you hadn't grabbed my shoulder, I wouldn't have *needed* to shout at you!'

'I was merely trying to warn you to keep still. You didn't, of course. You opened your mouth, ready to bawl me out—and kissing you seemed the best and quickest way to effectively shut it.'

'You could have simply *asked* me to be quiet. Or put a hand over my mouth.'

'Kissing you was safer than asking—and kinder than if I'd clapped a hand over your mouth.' His grin stretched. 'You still have very kissable lips, you know.'

She felt a momentary flutter—and dredged up a scowl to cover it, as annoyed with herself as with him. 'Well, don't try it again—even if a monstrous feral pig with bared teeth is charging me. You're likely to get a slap in the face.'

His grin turned wry, etching deep creases into his tanned cheeks. 'I guess I deserve that,' he said heavily, and she tensed, sensing that he wasn't referring to his kiss earlier, but to what had happened eighteen months ago.

'Don't let's get into past history,' she bit back, as bitterness quivered. 'As you said yourself, a lot of water has passed under the bridge since then.'

He nodded, his eyes suddenly bleak. 'Yes…a lifetime, in a way.' His shoulders slumped. 'I'm sorry, Tash—Nat,' he amended. 'I'm sorry I spoilt everything. I never meant to hurt you. That was the last thing I wanted. The last thing in the world.'

She bristled. 'Hurt me?' She lifted her chin, the proud glitter in her eyes covering the turmoil behind. 'If you think you left me eating my heart out for you, Tom, well, sorry.' Her chin rose a notch higher. 'You're not the only man in the world, you know. As I soon found out.'

The startled look in Tom's eyes gave her immense satisfaction…though it annoyed her at the same time. Did he think that, having known and loved *him*, she would never find another man who would spark her interest? The fact that she hadn't was neither here nor there!

'You've met someone else?' His voice cracked out.

Hostility flared in her eyes. She said steadily, with a shrug, 'I've met several men. Lovely men.' Warren the local pharmacist, Steve at the Art Gallery, Eddie, a young Brisbane artist. All charming, in their own way, but—

'But no one special?' Tom pressed, his eyes narrowing to glowing slits in the flickering firelight.

She swallowed. 'Warren's pretty special,' she lied with a flick of her shoulder. Warren was a dedicated pharmacist, and as solid as a rock. But hardly special. He lacked Tom's humour, Tom's adventurous spirit, Tom's— *Oh for heaven's sake, Natasha! Tom walked out on you!*

'He's decent and honest and totally dependable,' she asserted.

'Unlike me…uh?' Tom's brow lifted.

'That's right.' She dropped her gaze, her fingers

tightening round her half-empty tumbler. 'He's nothing like you in any way.'

'Is that why I'm here with you now and he isn't?'

Her head jerked up, her cheeks flaming. 'Warren's a busy pharmacist. He couldn't just leave his pharmacy.' She tried to imagine mild-mannered Warren camping out, roughing it in the wilds, being brave and protective, and couldn't. She would have had to protect *him*! 'Anyway, my *father*, if you recall, was supposed to come with me.' *Not you*, her eyes told him silently.

Tom raised his glass. 'Well, here's to you and Warren.' His eyes taunted her in the fire's soft glow. 'Though I take it you're not engaged *yet*.'

She shrugged, avoiding his eye. 'I rushed into one engagement. I'm not going to rush into another!' She gulped in a jagged breath. Rushed as their engagement had been, she'd had no doubts...none at all. Poor love-struck Natasha. *Tom* had been the one with the doubts.

'You're saying you rushed into our engagement without thinking?' His voice had dropped to a silken purr.

'Yes!' *I just wanted you. More fool me.* 'Engagements are romantic. Heady. Glamorous.' Scorn deepened the clear grey of her eyes. 'You swept me off my feet. The dashing outback pilot,' she mocked. 'The tough-guy Aussie adventurer.' Her lip twisted in self-derision. 'Because you shared my love of the bush and made me believe you shared the same ideals and values, you fooled me into thinking you were the man of my—' She snapped her mouth shut, cutting the rest off with a bitter snort.

Gulping down her rising resentment, she thrust out her chin to make her point. 'I'm not the same gullible, impetuous young innocent I was back then. I think before I do anything these days.'

'Very wise.' Tom's voice was somber, with no sign of self-satisfaction or mockery, his blue eyes a dark glitter in the firelight. 'Are you missing him, Natasha?' he asked softly. 'Did you call him from Jabaru? Is he missing *you*?'

She blinked, wondering for a second who he meant. Of course... *Warren!* He believed—

Swallowing hard, she reached down to brush something off her leg. She'd been out to dinner with Warren a couple of times, and that was it. She hadn't wanted to encourage him after the second occasion. He'd kissed her that night and his lips, his touch, had left her cold.

She bit down hard on her lip, thinking of the nights she and Tom had spent wrapped in each other's arms, lovingly, passionately entwined, their heated kisses sending them to the heights of—

She shut her eyes. Her experience with Tom

Scanlon should have been a salutary lesson! Passion was overrated. Passion could confuse you…blind you to reality. She had her head on straight these days.

Except when she was around Tom Scanlon!

'That's none of your business!' she bit out, and clamped her mouth shut, glowering into her glass. The conversation was getting dangerously out of hand, getting far too personal. 'You're forgetting the rules,' she reminded him sharply. 'No personal stuff…all right?'

'Damn the rules.' Tom's voice had roughened. Maybe the rum had roughened it. *Or her mention of another man?* 'Tash…Nat…damn it, it just doesn't feel right calling you Nat. But never mind that.' He seemed almost agitated—something she'd rarely seen in Tom, if ever. His jaw was clenched, his body taut, coiled like a spring, his eyes steely as they pierced hers in the glowing firelight.

'There's something I have to tell you,' he ground out. 'And it's not going to be easy…'

She tensed, eyeing him warily. 'You're in trouble with the police?' she quipped, seizing on flippancy to hide the heart-stopping apprehension that suddenly gripped her.

'I almost wish it were as simple as that.'

Alarm flared inside her. She stifled it, searing him with a withering glance. 'My goodness, what *can* it be?' she taunted, a faint tremor in her voice. 'You're engaged? You're married? You're divorced?' She gave a short, scathing laugh. 'You think that anything you have to tell me can affect me any more?'

She reached for Tom's flask of medicinal rum and recklessly dashed some more into her glass. 'Well, fire away,' she invited unsteadily.

As Tom hesitated, she found herself thinking wildly, irrelevantly, *Now I know what a pregnant pause is.* The still night air crackled between them. Her quickened heartbeat drummed in her ears. She realised she was holding her breath.

CHAPTER EIGHT

'I LIED to you, Tash,' Tom admitted finally. His tone was grave, his eyes bleak. This time he didn't apologise for using her old nickname, didn't even seem aware that he'd used it. 'Don't ask me why. I just panicked, I guess.'

Lied? Her hand trembled, almost spilling her rum. 'What do you mean—you lied to me? Lied about what?' Her eyes narrowed. Had he been two-timing her from the day they first met? Even while he was professing his undying love to *her* during their short-lived engagement?

'About getting involved with another woman in Sydney. About falling for someone else.' He leaned closer, as if to make sure she understood. 'I didn't even *meet* anyone else I'd have wanted to look at twice. In Sydney or anywhere else!'

Shock stopped the breath in her throat. He was lying! Not back then, but *now*. What was he up to? Why would he want to make her believe that the woman he'd dumped her for had never existed? Was this a clever ploy to win her back? A desperate, farcical ploy?

She took a deep shuddering breath before attempting to speak. Her throat felt like sandpaper, her lungs in grievous need of air. When she did finally answer, her voice was amazingly calm—belying the turmoil below.

'Not that it matters to me any more, but I don't believe you,' she said flatly. 'Only two days ago you told me "it didn't work out." And now you expect me to believe that the woman you dumped me for never existed in the first place? You're a liar, Tom Scanlon. A pathological liar. You can't help yourself!'

'I'm not lying now,' Tom said soberly. 'There never *was* another woman...not since you, Tash. I swear it. I'm just sorry I ever said there was!'

She drew in her lips, sucking in a shaky breath. 'Why would you tell me you'd met someone else if you hadn't? *It hit me like a bolt out of the blue*, you said.' Her eyes taunted him. 'You're saying you just made that up?'

Tom groaned aloud. 'Anything I said at the time was...' He broke off with a curse and shook his head. 'Hell, Tash, what have I done to you?'

She recoiled, her eyes turning to slivers of ice. 'You've done me a *favour*,' she flared, her voice a husky rasp. 'You cut the tie between us before I rushed into making the biggest mistake of my life. I'm *glad* you set me free,' she lied—though it wasn't really a lie because she'd tried desperately for the past eighteen months to believe that it *was* for the best, and had almost managed to convince herself.

She tossed her head, gripping her plastic tumbler like a lifeline. 'So don't insult my intelligence by—'

'But it's true, Natasha—there's never been anyone else. Not since the day I first met you.'

No 'Tash' this time, she noted shakily. It was as if he didn't want to risk provoking her, or upsetting her even more. His face was grimly earnest, the way she recalled seeing it last night at the camp site when he'd seemed about to say something and stopped. Had he tried to tell her then, and realised she wasn't in the mood to listen?

Well, she wasn't in the mood now!

'I'm turning in,' she growled, wishing she had a tent to crawl into, a door she could zip up to shut him out!

'Turn in, by all means, Natasha, but I'm still going to say what I need to say, and you'll have to listen—unless you want to sleep in the bush, away from the safety of the fire.'

'You're a bastard!' she breathed, her voice a ragged whisper.

'You're right,' he agreed heavily. 'But I didn't mean to be…honestly, Tash. I just wanted to set you free—and make sure you *knew* you were free.'

'You wanted to set yourself free, you mean!' Her eyes gleamed with contempt.

He bowed his head. 'All right…to set us both

free. I got cold feet,' he conceded. 'At the time I didn't think I could go through with it. Marriage…settling down…the whole *in sickness and in health, till death do us part* bit.' He shrugged his great shoulders, a pleading glitter in his eyes. 'You were so understanding on the phone when I called…promising to wait for me…offering to give me time…as much time as I needed. But I didn't think that time would change anything…not back then.'

He spread his hands, his eyes ruefully searching hers. 'I didn't want you waiting around, Tash, hoping I'd get it out of my system, expecting me to come back one day. I wanted to make a clean break and I…heard myself blurting out that I'd met someone else in Sydney. But it wasn't true, Tash—honestly. There's never been anyone but you.'

A bitter pain pierced her heart. 'You made me hate you!' Turbulent emotions—anger uppermost—throbbed in her voice.

'I *wanted* you to hate me,' Tom ground out. 'I didn't want you eating your heart out for me, or even thinking about me any more. At the time I didn't think I'd ever be back—I thought you'd be better off without me. My head wasn't on straight back then.'

'And you think it is now?' she spat back. 'You think that after all this time…after lying to me…humiliating me…*hurting* me…' Her voice wavered, the admission coming with difficulty. 'You think I'd want you back in my life now—even as a—a friend?' An involuntary tremor shook her.

She flicked him a sharp look. 'Or is it just forgiveness you're after?' she bit out. 'So that you can feel better about what you did to me?'

'No, Tash! Nothing could make me feel any better about what I did to you—'

'Then let's drop it, shall we? And you can drop the ''Tash'' too.' She injected a weary coldness into her voice, an icy indifference into her eyes—though it wasn't easy. 'You've confessed your sins. You can sleep at night now. Your conscience is clear.'

She gave a short, mirthless laugh. 'You simply got cold feet. It happens. You're not the first man to fear commitment, to panic at the thought of losing your freedom. You really didn't need to dream up another woman to convince me you wanted to be free of me, Tom. I'm sorry I was so p-pitiful and clingy that you thought you did.'

She took a deep gulp of her rum—too much, too quickly. She choked and began to cough.

Tom reached out a hand.

'Don't touch me!' She flinched away. Her teeth were chattering—with nervous tension, not from any drop in the temperature. This was intolerable! She had to get away from him—and fast. 'It's late,' she mumbled. 'I'm going to get some sleep.' She scrambled to her feet, dragging her sleeping bag with her. 'You can sleep on this side of the fire. I'll sleep on the other, between the fire and that mound of rocks.'

'As you wish.' There were no more apologies, no more pleas. No…that wouldn't be Tom's way. He'd said his piece and left her to digest it. Pleased with himself, no doubt, for getting it off his chest. 'Just be careful to tread heavily,' he warned, 'if you intend to make a trip into the bushes before turning in. You don't want to disturb any snakes.'

She shot him a searing glance before stomping off. 'Oh, don't worry, I've been learning fast how to deal with snakes.' But she made sure she did clomp heavily a moment later as she headed into the bushes, using her torch, not simply the moonlight, to illuminate her path—and also keeping an eye on the branches above. Snakes could also climb trees!

Before wriggling into the relative safety of her sleeping bag, she sprayed herself liberally with insect repellent—not that the mosquitoes were so bad here, with no water close by. It was more a symbolic gesture—to repel any unwanted approaches, from anything or any*one*.

She tried hard to settle down, but felt far too strung up to sleep. She couldn't stop shaking. Her mind was still reeling from this latest revelation. The 'other woman' who'd supposedly lured Tom away from her had never existed! Tom had made her up. He'd dreamed her up out of thin air, in a moment of so-called panic.

I wanted you to hate me, he'd said. Better to hate him than eat her heart out for him. She ground her teeth. Well, she *had* hated him. She'd never wanted to see him again. But she'd pined for him too...

She glowered into the dark folds of her sleeping bag. No doubt, having unburdened himself—having made his startling confession—he expected her to feel *better!*

Well, she didn't. She felt humiliated, all over again. It was degrading to think that he'd been so desperate to get her out of his life that he'd had to invent another woman to shake her off. It was *mortifying* to think he'd had to go to such ignominious lengths to get rid of her!

That was the most galling thought of all.

And what now? She muffled a moan. It was plain enough. Having tasted the precious freedom he'd wanted so badly, he'd had second thoughts and decided to come waltzing back into her life, as if nothing had happened, and turn it upside down again. Next he'd be expecting her to give him another chance. Another chance to hurt and humiliate her!

An owl hooted in the trees, its mournful call mocking her.

She buried her head deeper in her sleeping bag—only to jerk back, and then freeze, as a chilling howl echoed from somewhere deep in the bush. Another bloodcurdling howl followed.

Dingoes? She gulped, wishing she were lying closer to Tom. No, she didn't! At least she was lying, relatively protected, between the camp fire and a tumble of large sandstone rocks. She thought of Tom lying on the far side of the fire, with nothing to protect him from the dangers of the bush. But why should she care? She had nothing but contempt for him.

She groaned. She could hate him all she liked, but her arms still ached to hold him, her lips still longed to melt into the warmth of his. She'd dreamed about him many times at night…dreams that had tortured her the next day, when cold reality returned.

She'd thought he was out of her life for good, but now he was back, making confessions she'd never expected to hear, and she wasn't sure how to take…rousing feelings that only confused her more.

She writhed restlessly in her sleeping bag. If he had any thoughts about winning her back, he had no hope. No hope in the world. She wouldn't be that much of a fool. She'd be crazy to take him back and give him a chance to get cold feet again and walk out on her a second time. She wasn't as naive and trusting as she'd been eighteen months ago. She'd learned the hard way. She would never be a gullible pushover again.

She wasn't sure what time she finally fell asleep, or how long she slept, but her slumbers were cut short far too soon. A honeyeater's penetrating call woke her at dawn. She groaned and covered her ears, but the insistent notes hammered at her brain, spoiling any chance of sleeping in.

As Tom stirred at the same time, disturbing the cockatoos in the tree above him, even more raucous sounds split the air. Their ear-shattering screeches, as they hurled abuse at the human intruders, drowned out every other bird in the bush—even the strident, maniacal laughter of the kookaburras as they burst into furious cackling song at the same time.

Mercifully, the din only lasted a few minutes. By the time Natasha wriggled out of her sleeping bag, she could hear the whistling and warbling of the smaller birds again.

She stood up, stretching her cramped muscles.

'Good morning,' Tom called. He was already rolling up his bedding. 'Like some fruit and cracker biscuits for breakfast? It's about all I have to offer.'

At least he hadn't had the nerve to ask if she'd slept well!

'That'll do,' she said, coolly distant but polite. 'Then I'd like to start back. I want to be back at the camping ground well before lunchtime. We're driving to Yellow Waters, if you remember, and staying at Cooinda for a couple of nights.' There would be showers and toilets and fresh water at the camp site there, and other people around.

'Right. I can fill up on diesel at Cooinda and renew our supplies.'

'And I'll give my father a call,' Natasha decided aloud, flicking him a sharp look.

He didn't turn a hair. 'Right. Send him my best. I hope he's feeling better.'

If Charlie had ever been sick in the first place... Her brow darkened. She still found it almost impossible to believe that her father would be so underhand. But Tom Scanlon...well, he was a different kettle of fish. He'd be capable of anything. Even using subtle persuasion to twist Charlie's arm so that he'd agree to back out of his daughter's trip.

Neither of them touched on Tom's shock confession of the night before, either then or later in the day. Natasha remained coolly detached all the way back to their original camping site, where they'd left Tom's four-wheel-drive overnight. She thawed only slightly on the drive through the bush to Cooinda— and only to inquire about a particular bird or tree, or to ask Tom to stop while she took photographs.

They grabbed an early snack lunch at Cooinda, then while Tom was safely out of the way at the general store, she put a call through to her father. The phone rang for so long she was about to give up, thinking her aunt must be out shopping and her father still sick in bed, unable to answer. But then she heard a click and a gruff voice growling into the phone, 'Beale's Gallery.'

'Dad, you have your voice back!'

'Nat!' Was that surprise, pleasure, or caution in Charlie's voice? Or dismay that he'd answered the phone? He'd taken so long, he'd obviously thought twice about it! She didn't wait for him to ask how she was getting on with Tom Scanlon—though she knew he must be in a lather of suspense!

'How are you feeling, Dad? How's the gout? Why are you back in the gallery so soon? Where's Aunt Edith?'

He answered the easiest question first. 'Your aunt's popped out to pick up something from the pharmacy.'

The pharmacy... Natasha felt a twinge of guilt. *Warren's* pharmacy, Charlie was talking about. Poor Warren! If he only knew how she'd used him, making out to Tom that he was 'special'! Her father certainly didn't think Warren was special. He'd been relieved when she'd stopped seeing him. Charlie hadn't taken to the young pharmacist the way he'd taken to Tom. Reserved, serious-minded Warren wasn't dynamic enough, or engaging enough, she suspected, for Charlie's taste.

Or for hers, for that matter. But Tom Scanlon needn't know that!

'You need more medicine?' she asked her father, a worried frown creasing her brow. He couldn't be worse, could he? Surely he'd still be in bed if he was.

'Actually, Edith is picking up a prescription for herself. For her sinuses. Nat…how are you going, love?' Now a noticeable wariness had crept into his tone—and no wonder, she thought grimly. Having sent his unsuspecting daughter off on an intimate two-week camping trip with her ex-fiancé!

'Tell me how *you* are first, Dad,' she hedged. Let him sweat for a bit longer. He deserved it. 'When I spoke to Aunt Edith last you had laryngitis—on top of the flu and the gout. But you sound fine to me—you're even back in the gallery. Sounds like a very rapid recovery to me.' She paused, waiting for him to wriggle out of that, if indeed he had lied about being sick.

'The laryngitis was just one of those twenty-four hour things.' Charlie brushed it off. 'And the gout too. Those tablets the doc gave me the last time—'

'Yes, well, I'm glad you're feeling better, Charlie.' She still wasn't convinced that he'd been genuinely sick at all, but it was obvious he wasn't going to make any admissions—at least not at this point in time.

Maybe a more direct approach would catch him off guard.

'You had a nerve asking Tom Scanlon to take your place, Charlie,' she accused him. 'I can't believe you'd be so—'

'I knew he'd look after you, Nat,' he sliced in. 'He *is* looking after you, isn't he?' He sounded guarded again.

She drew in a quivery breath, thinking of the water buffalo yesterday, and Tom's reminders to drink more water, and the way he'd warned her about crocodiles on the evening she'd wanted to bathe in the billabong. She thought of the meals Tom had prepared for her and his intimate knowledge of the bush and its dangers—not only its dangers but its delights as well. She thought of his efficiency...his solid, reliable presence...his strength...

'That's beside the point,' she growled. 'You know what he did to me, Charlie, and what I think of him. And yet you—'

'He wanted a chance to sort things out, love.'

She caught her breath. 'So you did plan this...the two of you...'

A burst of coughing exploded in her ear. 'Sorry, love,' Charlie gasped out between coughs. 'Need my medicine.' Still coughing and sputtering, he choked, 'Give him a chance, Nat,' and hung up.

She stood where she was for a long, dumb-founded moment, suspicion warring with her natural sympathy. Was her father's bout of coughing gen-uine—or had he been putting on an act to avoid an interrogation?

'Well? How's your father? Did you get onto Warren too?'

She spun round. Tom had a faint swagger about him as he approached from the store, carrying supplies in each hand. His mouth, under the shady brim of his hat, was curved in a whimsical half-smile. She had a feeling he knew perfectly well that she hadn't been speaking to Warren.

'Warren works during the day.' She tried not to snap—or to sound defensive. 'I'd rather call him at night...when he's free to...talk.' She gave a suggestive little smirk of her own—wishing she could inject an equally provocative gleam into her eyes. Why couldn't she?

She stifled a sigh. Tom's pulsing vitality, his dynamic self-assurance, the taunting vibes flowing from his powerful frame, made it difficult to think of any other man, let alone pretend an interest she didn't feel.

'Have I been cramping your style, Natasha?' Tom arched an eyebrow. 'If you want to call your friend tonight, I promise I'll wander off into the bush so you can whisper your sweet nothings in private. As long as you promise to come to my rescue if any wild animals attack me.'

Her eyes flickered under his. Was he reminding her that they needed to stay close together at night, or just being his usual mocking self?

She remembered her father's phone call. 'I just spoke to my father,' she said levelly. 'He's made a remarkable recovery,' she added, eyeing him closely.

'Good for him. Told you he was a tough one.'

She pursed her lips. Not a trace of guilt or discomfort! But Tom was a master at duping people, she had to remember. He could lie at the drop of a hat.

Determined to show him she wasn't so easily fooled these days, she said recklessly, 'If I find out that you put my father up to this, Tom Scanlon, just so that you could wheedle your way back into my life…' She paused, her eyes pinning his, demanding an answer. Demanding the truth.

He met her gaze without flinching. 'Would it be so terrible if I did take some harmless steps to bring us closer again? We were close once…extremely close…until I stuffed everything up. A closeness like that is worth trying to find again.'

She trembled under the intensity of his piercing blue gaze. There was no mockery now, no evasion, no wariness. Nothing but a heart-jolting frankness.

'Then…you're admitting it?' she wavered. 'You and my father did—'

'I'd go to any lengths to make up for what I did to you, Natasha.'

Natasha, not Tash…not Nat. It shook her. As much as the admission he'd just made. She'd never known him to be so serious…so intense…so careful not to antagonise her!

She gulped in some air, her body trembling. Compressing her lips, she thrust out her jaw. 'I can't believe that my father would agree to such a devious, underhand, conniving, *insensitive* scheme!' Her voice throbbed with a mounting outrage. She'd had no say in the matter. None at all!

'I wanted to put right the harm I did to you, not to add to it,' Tom said gravely. 'Look… I'd better put these supplies in the fridge, before they melt in the heat. It's time we were on our way to Yellow Waters. You can take it up with me tonight.'

Tonight… Another night all alone with him— knowing now that he'd deliberately planned these two weeks alone with her…with her own father's collusion! She shook with a simmering fury…even as other deeper emotions quivered through her… emotions she didn't dare examine. She didn't want to know!

Once they reached the vast Yellow Water Billabong she had no time to brood over Tom's latest revelation. There was too much to do and see. While other tourists boarded a flat-bottomed boat for a guided cruise, Tom launched his aluminium dinghy and headed for the lily-covered flood plain.

It was even more spectacular than she'd been expecting.

Carpets of glorious lilies, in white, purple, pink and yellow, similar to the ones on her Monet

T-shirt, crowded among the green water plants. She'd never seen so many birds in one place—there were many that she'd never seen before, like the gregarious long-necked magpie geese and the red-crested lotus bird. She sucked in a delighted breath as she saw a red-crested lotus bird trotting easily across the lily pads on its huge stick-like feet.

While Tom fished for barramundi, the most sought-after fish in the North, she snapped madly with her camera. She'd brought her watercolour paints with her today, and was soon reaching for her folder of watercolour paper. As she lost herself in her painting, a wide-brimmed hat protecting her from the flood plain's burning heat, Tom had to keep reminding her to drink more water, more often.

Despite the hot, sultry air and the possibility of lurking crocodiles—and despite Tom's even more dangerous presence, dangerous to her emotions at any rate—she could feel her tension slipping away, bit by bit. Ducks glided past and terns swooped after tiny fish. Dragonflies zipped about in pursuit of insects, sunlight sparkling on their wings. Bees bumbled from flower to flower.

'The mozzies are mighty savage here,' Tom said, after a while. 'Maybe you should put some more repellent on.'

She'd been too busy drinking in the stunning beauty of the lily-covered billabong, in too much of a rush to record everything in watercolour and on film, to think about biting insects.

'Here... I'll do it for you.' Tom leant forward to spray repellent on her hands and ankles. Then he sprayed the palm of his hand and brushed it across her cheeks, brow and throat—with the gentlest of touches, almost like a caress.

'Thanks,' she breathed, shivering under his touch, oddly moved by his thoughtful gesture—yet peeved at the same time that she didn't find the touch of his fingers on her skin repugnant.

Disturbed by the realisation—when had she ever found his touch repugnant?—she turned away.

'Oh!' Her eyes widened. 'Look!' She pointed downward into the water. A sinister-looking crocodile was slinking through the lily pads, just under the surface.

'It's just a baby.' Tom's smile was indulgent— perhaps because she hadn't bitten his head off a moment ago when he'd touched her so tenderly.

'A *baby?*' she scoffed. 'It must be six feet long at least!'

'It'll probably grow another six, or even more,' Tom said, and added, quite unnecessarily, she thought, 'It's the ones you can't see that you have to worry about...the ones that stay well below the surface and can appear at any time—usually dramatically.'

She shuddered, feeling suddenly vulnerable in

Tom's open boat. Thank heaven it had an outboard motor!

Tom patted her knee. 'Just keep hoping they're feeling lazy and well-fed today, and don't cause us any trouble.'

Trouble? She shot him a sharp glance to see if he was joking. His lips were still curved in a half-smile, his eyes masked by his shady Akubra hat. She hoped he *was* joking. Surely the crocodiles wouldn't give any trouble if they stayed quietly in Tom's boat and weren't silly enough to climb out? She had no intention of even dragging a hand through the water!

As the afternoon wore on they glimpsed more crocodiles, some skulking among the lily pads of the flood plain, others—she began to lose count!—along the tree-lined river.

As they cruised further down the river, huge flocks of whistling ducks, seemingly undeterred by the presence of crocodiles, clustered thickly at the water's edge, their sharp whistles piercing the heavily humid air.

Natasha raised her camera and snapped furiously.

'Oh, Tom…look!' she breathed, pointing to a giant crocodile sunning itself on the river bank—a huge beast, perhaps fifteen feet long, fully visible from its long jagged jaws to its powerful tail.

She gulped at the size of it. 'Stop here!' she commanded in an urgent whisper. 'I want to paint this guy. I'll take some photos first, in case he decides to move away.'

The crocodile looked so lazy and docile as it basked in the dappled shade of the river bank that stories of crocodile attacks retreated to the back of her mind. After taking a few shots, she settled down to paint, while Tom sat contentedly fishing. He'd already caught a medium-sized barramundi, but kept hoping for the big one.

It was a tranquil, surprisingly companionable afternoon. There were long silences, but no words seemed necessary. Natasha tried to imagine her would-be suitor Warren coming with her on a painting trip and keeping himself occupied while she painted, but she couldn't. Fishing, camping and hiking had excited him about as much as his kisses had excited her!

'Hey, I've caught a real whopper this time!'

Tom's shout snapped her head round. She saw him exultantly reeling in his line. He was straining back in his seat, his feet braced against the side of the boat.

'Wow…would you take a look at *this* one!'

In a flash of gold, a gigantic barramundi broke the surface. As it thrashed about on the end of his line, Tom could barely hide his elation. 'If I land this one we'll have fish for a month!' he exulted as the powerful fish, gleaming silver now in the sunlight, fought with all its might to break free. It tried everything, even doing tail spins on the water. 'Whew! Mighty impressive! Hey, what the—'

There was an explosive upsurge of water from directly below the frantic barramundi. A huge crocodile, in a lightning movement, burst from the water and seized the great fish in its gaping jaws.

Natasha screamed.

CHAPTER NINE

As THE big crocodile sank back below the surface with its doomed prey, Tom's line went with it, dragging sharply on the fishing rod in his hand and almost pulling him into the water too.

The boat wobbled precariously as he fought to hold on.

Natasha instinctively reached out to grab him, tossing aside her folder and paints as she lunged forward to grasp his leg—the nearest part of him that offered a hold. She clung to his lower leg like grim death.

'Pull the knife from my belt!' Tom gasped. Both his hands were still occupied trying to save his straining fishing rod. 'We'll have to cut the line. I'm not losing this rod if I can help it!'

She let go of his leg and grasped him by his shirt, afraid he might still be dragged overboard if he released him altogether. With her free hand, she fumbled with the sheathed knife in his belt—keeping a wary eye on the spot where the crocodile had disappeared.

As she pulled out the knife, she sensed at once that something had changed. Tom, she realised, wasn't straining to hold the rod any more. The fierce jerking on the line had eased. The force of the crocodile had snapped the line!

She let out another scream as the crocodile rose vertically from the water in an explosive surge of power—even closer to the boat this time, so close that it showered water over them and rocked the boat to a dangerous degree.

This time it was Tom who grabbed *her*. He had both hands free now, having dropped his fishing rod into the bottom of the boat.

'It's all right, I won't let you fall in.' His eyes met hers briefly. 'We're not going to tip over.'

As the boat righted itself, they both watched the unfolding drama, fascinated yet tensely alert. The crocodile had the giant barramundi in its jaws. Before dropping back into the water, it gave a sudden twist of its scaly head and broke the huge fish in half.

Natasha's hand flew to her lips. Tom gave her arm a reassuring squeeze. 'Let's get out of here!' He released her and started up the engine. 'That's one greedy croc—and he obviously considers this his patch, damn it. No one will ever believe I caught a barramundi that size!'

As the engine roared to life and the boat shot forward, Tom took a wide detour around the spot where the crocodile was feasting on its prize. 'We'll head back to the billabong to catch the sunset.' He gave her a rallying smile. 'We won't have long to wait.'

By the time they reached the lily-covered flood plain, the sun was sinking behind the distant trees, turning the glassy water and the clear blue sky to a burnished gold. Unlike the noisy bustle of earlier in the day, a peaceful calm had settled over the water.

'This is magical,' Natasha breathed, grabbing her camera as a flock of magpie geese, silhouetted against the deepening orange sky, flew home to roost.

'Enough excitement for one day?' Tom asked as the brilliant colours of the sky gradually melted and rippled into the still water.

Turning to face him, she felt her heart miss a beat. He was looking at her in a way she hadn't seen before…not for eighteen months, at least. She wouldn't have tolerated that tenderness in his eyes before, wouldn't have *wanted* to see it, but now…

She gave herself a shake. She was just relieved that he was safe— relieved that the crocodile hadn't dragged him into the river…that was all it was!

'I don't suppose you took a photograph of that amazing barramundi I caught, before our gluttonous croc snatched it?' Tom asked hopefully. His eyes twinkled in the fading light. He knew perfectly well that she'd had no time to even think of taking a photograph. Everything had happened so quickly— and she'd been more intent on trying to save *him*.

'Sorry,' she said with a quick smile. 'I must have forgotten.'

'Do you realise that's the first time you've smiled at me—really smiled—since I came back into your life?'

She flushed, her smile wavering. *Back into your life?* How presumptuous of him…to think he was back in her life! She felt her hackles rise, but was in too benign a mood right now to take him to task.

'The look on your face when you lost your precious barramundi would make anyone smile,' she quipped, her smile turning wry.

'Well, I still have the other one I caught. We won't starve.'

'I don't think you'd ever starve, Tom Scanlon,' she said, giving praise where it was due. 'You'd live on fish, snakes and even witchetty grubs if you had to.' She reached for the cardboard folder containing the watercolour paintings she'd done that day—but it wasn't in the bottom of the boat. Her paints were there, and her notebook, but not her paintings.

She groaned as she realised what must have happened.

'What's wrong?' Tom asked, frowning.

'My folder of paintings…' She waved a hand. 'It went overboard, back along the river.'

He stared at her. 'You dropped your paintings *overboard?*'

Her eyes flickered under his. Why did *he* sound so upset? *She* was the one who ought to be upset. Her whole day's work was in that cardboard folder!

She tried to make light of it. 'I didn't even think about it when that crocodile appeared and you nearly—the boat nearly turned over,' she amended hastily. 'I just threw it down without even thinking.'

'To save *me*. You lost your day's work to save *me*.' Tom shook his head in wonder. 'That's very telling, you know…putting me ahead of your work.' His eyes gleamed as they met and held hers. 'You must feel something for me after all.'

'D-don't be silly. It was just a reflex action…when I thought you were about to fall overboard.' She could feel her cheeks burning, her breath catching. 'I didn't even think about it,' she insisted shakily.

'That's just it.' His eyes compelled hers, intense blue clashing with wary silver-grey. 'If you'd cared more for your work than for me, your reflex action would have been to save your paintings first, *then* me.'

She fumbled for her camera, raising it with trembling fingers. Anything to avoid his probing eyes!

'It's no big deal,' she muttered, busily snapping anything within range. 'I'll still have my sketches and photographs. I paint from photographs too, you know, and today I've taken a lot of snapshots, luckily. And I paint from memory too.'

'Yes…I remember.' His voice held a disturbing warmth. 'Fortunately, we were planned to come back first thing in the morning, if you recall, to watch the sunrise over Yellow Waters.' The eerie golden-yellow water at sunrise had given the Yellow Water Billabong its name. 'You can do your paintings again tomorrow, Tash. The crocs will still be here.'

'You—you're calling me Tash again.' Her voice was unsteady. She flicked her tongue over her lips, realising with a tremor that it didn't bother her so much any more. It had always been natural in the past for Tom to call her Tash—his own pet name for her—and it was starting to sound natural again.

'And you're beginning to accept it again…aren't you?' Tom said gently. But he didn't give her a chance to flare up again and deny it. 'We'd better start back. I don't want to be out here after dark.' With crocodiles around, he might have added, but didn't. 'Besides, I'm anxious to demonstrate my prowess at cooking fresh barramundi.' He licked his lips.

'You're anxious to *eat* it, more like,' she teased, her mouth watering already.

'Oh, I'm hungry all right,' he murmured, but he was looking at *her*, not at his day's catch, secure in the landing net at his feet.

She felt a tingly *frisson* at the wolfish gleam in his eye. For the first time she was tempted to respond to it. But she turned away quickly, reminding herself sharply what had happened the last time she'd responded to that hungry look in Tom Scanlon's eyes…during their ill-fated courtship. She'd lost her heart to him—her heart, body and soul—and he'd returned the favour by trampling her foolish heart beneath his feet.

'I thought we were heading back,' she growled. 'I'm ready for a long relaxing shower.'

She didn't chat on the way back to the landing stage. She concentrated on taking photos of the fading sunset instead.

She couldn't remember when she'd had a more delicious dinner. Fresh, delicate barramundi cooked in a blackened frypan with garlic, salt and pepper, sizzling onions and red peppers fresh from the hotplate, foil-baked potatoes, and boiled vegetables. To do the meal justice, Tom had produced a bottle of Chardonnay from his car frig.

As they sipped their wine, he lamented with a wry grin, 'I guess we should drink to the one that got away.' He held out his glass and touched it to hers.

'To the one that got away,' she said solemnly. 'Let's hope it was an old fish and as tough as old boots. It couldn't have been any more succulent than this one,' she consoled him. 'Don't you agree?'

'Very succulent.' He was looking at *her* again, in that same tender, highly disturbing way.

She dropped her gaze, her dark eyelashes fanning her cheeks. After he'd walked out on her she'd never expected to see that tender warmth again... hadn't *wanted* to see it again. She'd be mad to respond to it...to encourage him in any way. He could take fright again...get cold feet again...and she couldn't go through that pain, that devastation, a second time. She wouldn't!

'More wine, Tash?'

She shook her head, putting a hand over her glass. 'No thanks, no more for me.' Wine weakened her defences too much. And being weak and defenceless around Tom Scanlon was dangerous. 'It's making me thirsty. I'd rather have a glass of water.' She reached for the water bottle. She *was* thirsty, she realised. The humidity in the air had increased, and the temperature had barely dropped since the sun had gone down.

'I'll join you.' Tom pushed the cork back into the wine bottle and held out his empty glass for some water. 'We can have the rest of the wine tomorrow night, with some more of the fish.'

She blinked in surprise as she reached out to fill his glass with water. Tom Scanlon putting a cork back into an unfinished bottle of wine? It pushed her curiosity to its limit. 'This is some diet you're on,' she commented lightly. 'Only one glass of wine.'

His eyes glinted, twin pinpricks of gold in the firelight's glow. 'I'm trying to keep my weight down and stay healthy.'

Involuntarily, her gaze swept over him. A fitter man she had yet to see! Trim, taut, terrific—and sexy as hell! 'Your father's death must have given you an awful fright,' she mused aloud, hoping he'd open up about his father and tell her more about the rift between them.

'It did come as a shock. But I'd already started on my diet months before my father died.' He paused. 'Not long after I arrived in Sydney, in fact.'

Not long after he'd arrived in Sydney? After breaking off his engagement? She found she was holding her breath, wondering what had prompted such a radical change.

Perhaps some woman he'd met in Sydney had laughed at him, spurring him to do something about his weight and his bad eating habits. It could be as simple as that. A matter of hurt pride.

She tightened her lips and switched the subject, asking curiously, 'What made you start up an out-back safari business?'

He gave her a long considering look. 'I wanted to prove something to myself.'

'Oh? And did you?' He'd wanted to prove that

he could make his outback tours work…work and prosper. Was that what he meant?

'Yes…I did, as a matter of fact.'

Something in his tone suggested there was more to it than just money and success. She asked tentatively, 'Were you also trying to prove something…to your father?'

As his eyes flickered at the mention of his father, she asked impulsively, 'What *did* happen between you and your father, Tom? It wasn't simply that you didn't get on with your new stepmother…was it?'

Tom jerked a muscular shoulder. 'No…that was just the last straw. My father and I never saw eye to eye. Different basic values, different ideals. He wanted me to follow him into the family business.'

'You never did tell me what kind of business your father was in,' she reminded him gently. Tom had never wanted to talk about it.

'My father owned an extremely successful confectionery business in Newcastle. When I told him I wanted to work on the land, not in a city office running a chain of factories, he blew his top. I stuck to my guns, and he finally agreed to let me do my own thing—hoping I'd get it out of my system, I guess—on the condition I did a university degree first, as a backup. I reckoned an agricultural course would come in handy when I owned my own cattle station, so I did Agricultural Science and Economics.'

His old dream to buy a cattle station…what had happened to it? When they were together eighteen months ago he'd been working virtually round the clock to save enough money to buy a property— even a run-down property that he could build up. He'd let her believe that he was keen to settle down…with *her*. Only he'd taken fright. He'd wanted his freedom more.

And he'd ended up starting an outback safari business instead.

'After a few years of working at all kinds of jobs and learning to fly a helicopter, my father told me he'd given me enough time doing ''other things'' and it was time I knuckled down to some ''real work''. He wanted me in the family business—and he wanted me there full-time, to learn the ropes so that I could take over from him when the time came. He even offered to step aside early and let me run the business myself. I'd be the boss, he said, and he'd merely advise.'

His mouth twisted. 'Even if I'd been tempted by the offer, I wouldn't have wanted my father breathing down my neck. We'd never held the same view on anything, and it was far worse after he married Meryl. When I made it clear I still wasn't interested and never would be, we had a blazing row. He said if I wouldn't go into the business then and there he never wanted to see or hear from me again. He'd disinherit me and I wouldn't get a cent.

'I told him he could keep his business and his inheritance, and I walked out. I took up helicopter flying with a vengeance—mustering cattle, flying tourists around, whatever jobs paid best—determined to make as much money as I could as quickly as I could. I wanted to show my father I could make my own way in the world, that I didn't need anything from him.'

'So that's what drove you,' Natasha whispered, her spirits dipping. 'The cattle station wasn't so much a dream as a—a means to an end. To show your father that you could be as successful as he was.'

'No!' Tom denied sharply. 'I wanted it for *me*. That was the kind of life I'd always wanted—owning and running my own property. And once I met you, Tash, I wanted it for you too. It's what I still want.'

Her heart fluttered. *Still want.* Was he planning to sell his safari business to buy some land to start up a cattle station? Hoping she'd relent and take him back?

He leaned forward, catching her hand. 'When I met you, Tash, I became more determined than ever to make something of my life. That's why I took on extra flying jobs and worked at such a furious pace…not looking after myself. My life became a mess.'

Her hand froze in his. So Tom thought of his life

back then—with her—as a mess! A stabbing hurt pierced her. She thought of the callous way he'd walked out on her, and tugged her hand free, her eyes hardening.

'And you never tried to see your father again after that?' she asked, turning the focus away from herself, to put distance between them. If Tom thought she was going to fall back into his arms the moment he clicked his fingers, he could think again!

'No. He'd told me not to darken his door again unless I changed my mind. I never did. Neither of us backed down. Too stubborn.' His lip twitched. 'I was like him there, I guess. I did send him a card each Christmas and on his sixtieth birthday, just to let him know I was still alive.'

And still thinking of him, Natasha wanted to add, but kept silent, not wanting him to stop now.

'He never acknowledged any of them,' Tom said heavily. 'And then I heard that he'd died.'

His voice had changed, she noticed, thickening with an emotion that stirred a wave of sympathy. He'd lost his chance to make up with his father. Two stubborn men, never healing their bitter rift.

She almost reached out to him, but stopped herself in time.

'So…' She cleared her throat. 'What happened to your father's confectionery business? Is your stepmother running it now?'

'Hardly. No… Dad sold the business before he

died. He'd found out he had a heart condition and decided to retire and enjoy what was left of his life. My stepmother wanted to travel…spend…live it up. The pace was too much for my father.' He seemed about to say something else, but hesitated, as if seeking the right words.

As the silence lengthened, Natasha's heart went out to him. Perhaps it was too painful.

To spare him, she sought a diversion. It wasn't too difficult to find one.

'Ouch!' She slapped her leg. 'These mozzies are killing me. They're biting me through my jeans!'

'Yes, they're bad tonight.' Tom seemed to sigh as he unfolded his long frame and rose to his feet. 'This heavy humidity isn't helping. You'd better turn in, Tash—it's getting late. I'll clear up here.'

She jumped up. She'd already put up her tent, while Tom was cooking dinner. 'What about you?' she asked, pausing. 'You'll sleep under a mosquito net, won't you?'

He cocked his head at her. 'For a minute there I thought you were going to invite me to share your tent.' He gave a chuckle at the affronted look on her face. 'Don't worry about me. Mozzies don't find me as succulent as they obviously find you.' His eyes met hers. She quivered under the blatant message in the glittering depths.

She ran her tongue over her lips, recalling what

he'd said earlier, back on the river. *You must feel something for me after all.*

She gulped down a lump in her throat. If Tom only knew… If he only knew that she'd never stopped feeling something for him, hurt as she'd been…as she still was, deep down. Would it make him even bolder if he knew?

She didn't wait around to find out.

Ten minutes later she was sprawled out on top of her sleeping bag—it was too hot and sultry to snuggle inside—smothered in insect repellent to deter any mosquitoes that might have flown into the tent before she'd zipped up the door.

Poor Tom, sleeping out in the open, at the mercy of the mozzies… She wondered if he had a mosquito net over him.

Tom can look after himself, she thought, a surge of heat prickling her cheeks. I'm not inviting him in here!

It must have been another hour before she finally drifted off to sleep.

CHAPTER TEN

IN THE early hours of the morning she woke with a start.

There was a terrible din outside the tent. Rain! Teeming rain. Rain like she'd never heard before, drumming into the parched earth and the flimsy tent covering her.

But that wasn't the only sound…there was another, just outside the zipped-up door of her tent. It was muffled by the din, but identifiable.

A man's voice.

Tom's voice!

'Natasha, wake up, damn it. Let me in. I'm drowning out here!'

'Oh!' She scrambled to her feet, fumbling for the zipper in the darkness, not thinking twice about giving him sanctuary. Not having *time* to think twice. Not that she would have dreamed of refusing him. Who could survive out there?

'Come on! What are you *doing?*' Tom shouted over the clamour.

'Give me time. It's dark in here.'

'You've a torch, haven't you?'

'You want me to find the torch or find the zipper that'll open this door?'

'I don't care, just hurry!'

'I'm *trying* to. Ah…got it!' She found the zipper and pulled. Before the door was fully open Tom was thrusting his way in, his bowed frame brushing past her. 'Ugh!' she leapt back. 'You're soaked!'

'Sorry. Want me to take them off?'

'No!' Alarm sharpened her voice. Not that she'd be able to see anything if he did—it was pitch dark inside the tent.

'You don't care if I catch pneumonia?' Beneath the plaintive note in his voice was a glimmer of amusement. Even a hint of jubilation.

Because he was safely out of the rain? Or—she swallowed—because he was here inside her tent…alone with her?

'You won't catch pneumonia in this heat,' she scoffed. She winced at the way her teeth were chattering—and it certainly wasn't from the cold. The air in here was positively steamy! In more ways than one.

'Better zip up the door again before the mozzies get in. I'll do it,' Tom offered. 'There…got it.' He turned round—with difficulty. There was barely room for the two of them to stand. She could feel his damp warmth every time she moved, as she tried frantically, unsuccessfully, to put some distance between them.

'I thought this was the dry season,' she said shakily. Her eyes were finally becoming accustomed to the darkness and she could make out his shape now, dark and shadowy, looming over her.

'It's the *early* dry season,' Tom said. 'You can still get the odd tropical downpour at this time of year. Either an overnight deluge lasting a few hours...or it could go on for days.'

'Days!' She groaned. Well, she certainly wasn't sharing her tent with Tom Scanlon for more than one night. No way!

Tom's voice cut through the din. 'There would be more room if we both sat down.'

'Right.' She plonked herself down immediately, drawing the edge of her sleeping bag back towards her, so it wouldn't get wet. But when Tom shuffled round to find a space, he stumbled over something—the torch she couldn't find, perhaps?—and sprawled full-length to the floor, landing, with a growled curse, on top of her!

She squealed, rolling back onto her sleeping bag under his considerable weight. She lay there helplessly, flat on her back, with his powerful frame pressing into her quivering softness, his soaked body moulding to her shape. His heat and dampness were flowing through her shirt and jeans, making her as moist and clammy as he was. Thank heaven she'd gone to bed fully dressed!

As she struggled for breath, she felt *his* breath, hot over hers. She went still. He went still too. She expected him to laugh, to apologise, and roll away from her, but he didn't. With her still pinned beneath him, he brought his mouth down hard on hers…hungrily, like a starving animal, devouring her lips as if he needed them to stay alive.

A searing hot flame licked down her body. Her bones melted, all fight ebbing away as a fierce longing welled inside her, overpowering her. She opened her mouth and began kissing him back with the same wild desperation, as eager as he to assuage the thirst that had been building, bit by feverish bit, over the past couple of days…frantic to savour the lips that had once clung to hers with a burning passion…

With love and passion.

She groaned under the scorching fire of his lips. The passion was still there…but love? Had Tom ever truly loved her? If he had, how could he have walked away from her?

She wiped such torturous thoughts from her mind, clinging to him, aching for him, powerless to pull away. She didn't care any more! She couldn't let him go, *wouldn't* let him go. She wanted him…needed him. She couldn't worry about anything else now.

'Tash…' Tom lifted his head slightly, as if he'd sensed her turmoil and wanted to reassure her. Bringing up a hand, he brushed the tips of his fingers over her parted lips with infinite gentleness. 'If you knew how much I've missed these lips…

missed *you.* The last eighteen months have been pure hell. I never stopped wanting you, Tash... dreaming of you...*burning* for you. It's been sheer agony without you.'

Sheer agony? She stared up at him dazedly.

He pressed his lips into the softness of hers, drawing back just far enough to murmur, 'You want me too, don't you...just as much? Even after what I did to you?' He didn't mention love, as if afraid to. 'It can be the same for us again, Tash, if you'll give me a chance...a chance to explain...'

Explain? What did he have to explain? Was there *more?*

She shifted in his arms. She didn't want explanations...not *now.* Why didn't he just kiss her? Couldn't he see that she was burning for him, offering herself to him? They could talk later.

'Later,' she breathed, silencing his lips with her own. At once the fire between them ignited again, and she was lost in the ravaging heat of his kisses. She moaned, straining against him, her veins turning to fire, her breath quickening, rasping in her throat.

In his arms like this, being kissed like this, she was powerless to think, let alone to care about explanations. She was in a mindless state of hot, pulsing excitement, lost to reality—other than the reality of the man holding her, the lips hungrily devouring hers.

She felt his warm hand on her breast, cupping its heaving fullness, his fingers gently kneading the soft flesh. The sensitive peak tingled, hardening as she pressed wildly against him, wanting more, showing him she wanted more, as much as he wanted to give.

'I've dreamed of this, Tash,' he growled against her lips. 'Of having you back in my arms again…where you belong.'

Did she? She moaned, not wanting to talk, or even to think. Only wanting to feel, to forget that a year and a half ago he'd walked out on her. She clung to him, smothering his lips with the frantic need of her own.

As their passion soared, the rain continued to thud down on the tiny tent, while outside the water rose, swirling round them, soaking into the parched earth.

Then, as suddenly as it began, the deafening deluge stopped.

Tom gave an uncaring grunt, moving his body over hers until she was moaning and writhing in ecstasy, arching against him in spasms of exquisite pleasure.

And then a shrill sound pierced the heavy night air.

A bloodcurdling scream.

Natasha's head jerked back. 'W-what's *that?*'

Her voice was a husky whisper. 'A dingo? A wild pig?'

'That's no animal.' Tom was already setting her aside—gently, reluctantly—and struggling to his feet. She heard him cursing as he sought the catch to open the tent door. Once found, he had it open in a flash. Then he was gone.

Scrambling to her feet, she plunged out after him, her bare feet splashing through water almost up to her ankles. A few more seconds and it would have been inside the tent.

Torches were flashing and other lights springing on. As she ran past Tom's four-wheel-drive, she saw people gathered around another big vehicle parked at the far end of the camping ground. At once she saw why. A huge branch lay across the vehicle, crushing the roof. A woman was in hysterics nearby, being comforted by other campers.

'Why is that woman screaming?' she asked one of them as she approached. 'Is there someone inside the car?'

'Yes, her husband. He's trapped—but still alive, thank heaven. His wife was sleeping in a tent, luckily.'

Natasha swallowed hard. She'd been sleeping in a tent while Tom had been lying out in the open. What if a branch had fallen on *him*? She shuddered. How could she bear to lose him now, just when they

were beginning to heal the bitter hurts of the past
year and a half?

Tom was helping a group of campers to remove
the buckled door of the mangled vehicle and ease
the trapped man out. By some miracle the lucky
man, who'd been lying asleep on a rear seat, hadn't
been crushed or seriously hurt, despite the roof almost squashing him. He only needed help to crawl
out. He had a few scratches, that was all. But his
big four-wheel-drive wouldn't be going anywhere—
not until a tow truck came to haul it away.

A sorry end to a camping tour, Natasha thought,
feeling for them.

With the shocked man and his wife both being
cared for by friends, one of whom happened to be
a doctor, and someone else calling for the ranger
and a tow truck, Tom strode over to her, urging her
to go back to bed.

'You'd better try to get some sleep. We've an
early start, remember.' There was regret in his
voice. And a tenderness that shook through her from
head to toe. 'I'll help to clear away the tree, then
spend the rest of the night in the back seat of the
car.' He jerked a thumb in the direction of his four-
wheel-drive.

She slanted him a look. Why hadn't he taken ref-
uge in his big four-wheel-drive in the first place,
when the downpour began, rather than squeezing
into her poky two-man tent, which was really only

suitable, comfortably, for one? He would have had far more room in his big sturdy vehicle.

Tom's eyes glittered in the darkness, as if he knew what she was thinking. As if it amused him. But he made no comment. She wondered if he'd made a dive for her tent without even thinking, simply because it was the closest haven and he'd been desperate to get out of the teeming rain, quick smart.

Or had he thought only too well?

A quiver ran through her. What would have happened, she wondered, her skin heating again, if that branch hadn't fallen…if that woman hadn't screamed? Would Tom have gone on making sizzling, passionate love to her? She wouldn't have stopped him. She'd been in a state of overheated, mind-numbing ecstasy, ready to combust.

Could she have survived a night of passion with the man who'd hurt her once and could so easily hurt her again? Tom was the only man she'd ever loved—and she loved him still, despite the bitter hurt he'd inflicted on her in the past. But what if all he felt for her was lust? What if all he wanted was a short-lived affair, before taking off again? How would she ever get over him a second time?

It can be the same for us again, he'd said. *If you'll give me a chance…a chance to explain.*

To explain *what?* She hadn't wanted to listen. Not then. But sometime tomorrow, she thought, however bad it was, however difficult to hear, or to bear, she had to know. Everything. She wanted no more secrets between them.

No matter what those secrets were.

CHAPTER ELEVEN

SHE was sleeping so soundly that even the persistent chirping and squawking of the birds didn't rouse her at dawn. It was the brightness of the morning sun that eventually woke her, as its sharp rays penetrated the door of her tent.

She groaned, wanting to sink back into her pleasant slumbers. Into her pleasant dreams…

The *sun?*

Cursing as she realised it was well after sunrise, she stumbled from her tent, wondering why Tom hadn't woken her. They'd missed the sunrise over Yellow Waters! Not that it greatly bothered her, she realised, as memories of last night flooded back. She was more anxious to hear whatever it was Tom had to tell her. *A chance to explain*, he'd said. She pressed a shaky hand to her chest.

She found him leaning against the door of his four-wheel-drive, making a call on his mobile phone—though he brought it to a halt the moment he saw her. 'Right, Jane…see you shortly. Look forward to it. Bye!'

Jane? Her steps faltered. Was 'Jane' the reason he hadn't woken her? Because he'd wanted to call this woman in secret? *See you shortly*, he'd said. Not 'soon,' or 'when I get back,' but 'shortly.' 'Shortly' could mean now, today!

'Good morning.' Her voice was hoarse, uncertainty coiling through her. She looked up at him, waiting for an explanation.

Give me a chance to explain, he'd said last night. Her heart skipped a beat. Was his explanation something to do with the woman he'd just been speaking to?

'Ah, Tash…a slight change of plan. You won't mind putting off our trip to Yellow Waters for one day, will you? We've missed the sunrise today anyway.'

She flicked her tongue over dry lips. 'No…of course not.' For once her painting seemed unimportant…an irrelevance…a hindrance even. 'You wanted a chance to—to explain something to me.' Whatever it was, she had to know, and to know now…this morning!

'That's right.' Tom's eyes gave nothing away. 'But we have someone to meet first. Grab a bite to eat, Tash, while I pack up the tent and clear up.'

Someone to meet… She swallowed. He wanted *her* to meet this woman he was looking forward to seeing again? Who *was* she?

'All right,' she mumbled. She didn't feel a bit hungry, but maybe some food would give her the strength to cope with whatever she had to face.

While she gulped down some fruit, which was all she felt like, Tom cleared up the camping site. The rain had long since gone, leaving a perfectly clear blue sky, but drops of pearly water still glistened on the leaves, and the fragrance of freshened grasses and damp earth drifted in the air.

'Ready to go?' Tom asked, and she nodded, pausing only to ask after the man who'd been crushed in his car.

'His friends have driven him back to Darwin for some precautionary X-rays. He was still a bit shocked and bruised, but otherwise he seemed okay. The tow truck came during the night and carted off his four-wheel-drive.'

'I'm glad he's all right,' she said with feeling. It was an accident that could happen to any camper, if parked too close to large trees. 'Um…where are we meeting this person you mentioned?' She tried to look unconcerned, but her throat felt as dry as desert sand.

'At Jabaru,' Tom said briefly, leaning into the rear seat to fill their flasks with cold water from his car frig. 'Hop in!'

She hauled herself up into the passenger seat. Jabaru? She chewed on her lip as she waited for him to climb in beside her. All the tourists buses came into Jabaru…

Was this friend coming by bus from Darwin?

She couldn't be anyone important to him! *It's*

been sheer agony without you, Tash, he'd told her only last night. Jane was probably his secretary…or one of the tourist guides who worked for him. But Natasha could not understand why he was being so secretive about it. Maybe she had read too much into last night. After all, it had been a wildly spontaneous act of sheer animal passion, ignited by unusual circumstances—the unexpected downpour, Tom tumbling on top of her, the steamy tropical heat.

Tom hadn't said he loved her. He'd spoken of wanting her, of missing her, of her belonging in his arms. Was that love? Or was it just passion—*lust?* Was that all he felt for her? All he'd ever felt for her?

She shifted in her seat, chafing to find out precisely what he did feel for her… She felt impatient and apprehensive, afraid of the secrets he was still holding back.

'Well, come on, are we going or not?' she asked edgily.

Tom threw her a grin as he swung himself into the seat beside her. 'Your wish, my adorable Tash, is my command,' he said, and she wondered, a trifle wistfully, if it really was—and if wishes ever came true.

My adorable Tash… It could be simply a flirty, throwaway endearment. Or did he truly adore her…now that he'd had eighteen months of freedom to get the wanderlust out of his system? *It can be the same for us again*, he'd promised last night, *if you'll give me a chance to explain.*

But he wanted her to meet someone first. A tremor riffled through her.

She barely spoke on the way to Jabaru. She was too tense, her entire body a jangle of nerves. Tom barely spoke either, his brow knitted as he concentrated on his driving. He seemed tense himself, she thought...far from his usual relaxed, confident self. It made her more jumpy than ever.

Instead of driving into the township of Jabaru, as she'd expected, Tom drove on to Jabaru's small airport. Was the mysterious Jane arriving by plane?

But it wasn't a woman who met them at the airport. It was a young man in a short-sleeved shirt with winged epaulets on his shoulders, and a cap with similar wings. A pilot!

'Jacko!' Tom greeted him. 'How are you, mate?'

'Tom...good to see you.' A wide grin slashed the young pilot's deeply tanned face. 'And this is our charming passenger, I take it?' Bold dark eyes swept over Natasha, but she couldn't take offence—not with that good-humoured smile and those warm twinkling eyes.

His words sank in. *Passenger?* She blinked.

'Yep...this is Natasha.' Tom grinned back. It was obvious he'd already mentioned her to Jacko—perhaps on the phone earlier. 'Natasha, this roving-eyed reprobate is an old friend of mine, Dave Jackson—who only answers to Jacko. He's the man I wanted you to meet…' Something shimmered in his blue eyes. 'He's got a surprise in store for you. Ready to go, Jacko?'

'Ready as I'll ever be. Follow me.' Jacko led them across the tarmac to a twin-engined Cessna with the words Jacko's Scenic Flights emblazoned on the side.

'Your flight, ma'am,' Jacko said, grinning at Natasha.

A scenic flight! She looked up at Tom with glowing eyes. 'Tom! You've arranged for me to see Kakadu from the air!' Jane, she thought in swift shame, must have been the airport attendant who'd booked the flight for him. *See you shortly*, Tom had said. At the airport! She grimaced at her own stupidity. Her lack of trust.

She must start trusting Tom again or there'd be no hope for them.

'What a wonderful idea!' she cried. A bird's eye view from a small plane would give Kakadu a whole new dimension, providing a dramatic panoramic overview and putting it all into perspective.

Tom merely smiled, and helped her aboard.

Jacko winked at Natasha as they settled into their seats. 'Welcome to the flight of a lifetime, Natasha.'

She felt a flutter, part excitement, part apprehension. *The flight of a lifetime* had a daredevil ring about it. She just hoped Jacko wasn't a crazy, daredevil pilot.

She caught Tom's eye. He'd been a pretty adventurous pilot himself when he'd been flying helicopters, but he'd always been competent and in control. She'd always felt safe with him. But Jacko she knew nothing about.

Tom smiled reassuringly.

As the engine roared to life, she glanced round at the four empty seats behind. She nudged Tom. 'Are we the only passengers?' she asked in surprise.

'Looks like it,' Tom said coolly. 'Sit back and enjoy the ride, Tash.'

The Cessna was already rolling down the runway. She held her breath, gripping her seat as the small plane soared into the air. Tom's hand, big and comforting, closed over hers.

'You can relax—Jacko's an ace pilot,' he assured her, the warmth of his hand easing her tension as nothing else could. 'Look down below,' he said a moment later.

'Ooh,' she breathed as she turned to look. The spectacular shapes and mighty sandstone cliffs of the Arnhem Land Escarpment lay below. Patches of water, high up in the rocks, gleamed in the sunlight. There were even a few waterfalls after last night's deluge.

The stunning panorama, and Tom's reassuring presence beside her, quickly calmed any fears—

even when the plane banked sharply to provide a closer view. Jacko was obviously an experienced pilot, every bit as capable as Tom.

She sat back and enjoyed the unfolding views as they swept over rivers and wetlands, over woodland plains and glistening billabongs. Then after a while it dawned on her that they'd left Kakadu Park behind. They were heading south.

She flicked a look round at Tom. 'Where are we going? There's a cattle station down below!'

The corner of his lip tweaked. 'There are a lot of cattle stations in the Northern Territory.' His eyes danced. 'Jacko does cattle station tours as well as scenic Top End tours. I thought you might like to see one at close quarters.'

'Oh…fine.' She searched his face. Tom had once flown tourists to cattle stations himself, in his helicopter flying days. He'd also flown tourists to the far North's top scenic spots, and mustered cattle by helicopter. She wondered if he missed his hectic life as a helicopter pilot.

She heard herself asking him, 'Do you miss flying, Tom?'

'I've only ever missed you, Tash,' he said without hesitation, and she felt her heart constrict, wishing she could believe him. But how could she, when he'd stayed away from her for so long without a single word?

'But talking of flying,' Tom added smoothly,

changing the subject almost too quickly, 'it's in my blood, I guess. I'm thinking of buying a small plane—maybe a Cessna, like Jacko's.'

'You—you are?' So he had no plans as yet to buy a cattle station. He preferred the outback safari tour business. 'You're planning to do scenic flights like Jacko? Does that mean you'll be giving up your four-wheel-drive tours?'

'Oh, no, I'll still keep on running those,' Tom said easily, an amused glimmer in his eyes. 'But I won't be doing scenic flights... Ah! Here we are.' He drew her attention back to the scene below. 'This is the cattle station we've come to visit. What do you think of it?'

She glanced down at the vast rolling plain below. It seemed to go on forever. Cattle were clearly visible...lots of cattle. A narrow river meandered through the partially timbered property. As they swooped low she saw outhouses...sheds...cattle pens. A tree-lined drive led to an oasis-like garden and a bungalow-style homestead, its iron roof gleaming in the midday sunlight. There was even a tennis court and a swimming pool. Another smaller house stood nearly, nestled into another patch of green.

Quite a property, she thought. Why would it matter to Tom what she thought of it? Perhaps he still had a hankering to buy a cattle station after all, and wanted to find out if she was still interested herself. Perhaps he was even thinking of buying this one!

She smiled pensively. An entrancing thought... but how could Tom afford a magnificent property like this—or any property, for that matter—if he was planning to buy a plane? Buying and running a light plane would cost a packet!

Still, it was pleasant to daydream. Tom, she thought wistfully, had taught her to dream...to share *his* dream. Only his dream, surely, was out of reach now. Buying a small plane would be nothing compared to buying a thriving cattle station—like the one down below.

Besides, the dream that Tom had once shared with her, before he'd given up helicopter flying to take on 'new challenges', had been a far more modest dream. He'd planned to buy some land or a run-down property that was going cheap and build it up into a going concern over time.

The cattle station they were about to visit was already well-established. It looked extremely prosperous, and was probably worth a fortune. It would be far out of Tom's reach—even if he sold his safari business, which he'd just told her he didn't intend to do.

But looking over the property might give Tom ideas for the future. Perhaps that was it.

She tensed as the plane swooped down towards the small dirt airstrip. As it taxied to a halt Tom leaned towards her. 'Hungry? I hope so. They've invited us to lunch.'

'Oh! That's kind of them.' Outback people were very hospitable, she thought. Even to paying tourists. Or was Tom—or Jacko—a friend of the owner? She had no time to ask as Jacko ushered them both out. A young dark-haired woman was hurrying across the airstrip towards the plane.

'Jane!' Tom strode forward with arms outstretched. 'Good to see you.'

Jane? Natasha's jaw dropped. The woman he'd spoken to on the phone earlier *owned* this magnificent spread? Or was the daughter of the owner?

She gulped as she took in the girl's breezy smile, her lively dark eyes, her tall willowy figure, watching dazedly as Tom gripped the girl by the shoulders and planted a warm kiss on her healthily suntanned cheek.

Her stomach knotted. They obviously knew each other—and knew each other well. *How* well? she wondered shakily.

Tom turned, catching her hand. 'Natasha, I'd like you to meet Jane. Natasha Beale…Jane Thomas,' he said formally.

'Lovely to meet you, Natasha,' Jane said warmly. 'Did you have an enjoyable flight?'

'Very pleasant, thanks.' Natasha smiled—a smile that came surprisingly easily. She wished there was something she could dislike about Jane but there wasn't. The girl was warm, open and friendly, with a bright, bubbly personality. And very attractive. She had the sort of face it would be a pleasure to paint.

She shook off the startling thought. *What did Jane mean to Tom?* That was all that mattered!

'I've prepared lunch for you,' Jane said. 'Why don't you go on ahead to the homestead, Tom, and show Natasha round the garden while I help Jacko refuel the plane? We'll join you shortly.' Her eyes twinkled at Tom—almost as if they shared a secret, Natasha thought with a dip of her spirits. Or was she just imagining it? Jealousy could play strange tricks.

Was she jealous? Did she have *reason* to be jealous? *There's never been anyone but you, Tash*, he'd assured her. *I've dreamed of having you in my arms again…where you belong.* If only she could believe him!

'Fine…see you, Jane.' Tom drew her away. His blue eyes, squinting against the harsh midday sun, were unreadable.

She felt a ripple of foreboding. *A chance to explain*, he'd said. To explain about Jane, did he mean? Did he want to make it clear that they were friends—good friends—but there was nothing more to it than that? Or at least…not any more?

A painful ache curled through her. *It's been sheer agony without you*, he'd told her. But had Jane helped to ease that agony during the long months he'd been struggling with his demons?

It was only a short walk to the homestead, across an expanse of baked earth and dry grass. With the hot sun beating down on them they passed through a small picket gate into an amazingly profuse garden of bouganvillea, roses, frangipani and other flowering shrubs. Tall tropical palms cast welcome shade over the green lawns and the inviting-looking homestead, with its screened verandah.

Tom steered her to a garden seat in a shady corner of the garden.

'Jane's kindly allowing us some time to talk before we have lunch,' he drawled. He still had hold of her hand, and gave it a slight squeeze, as if to reassure her.

It didn't. 'You've discussed our—our problems with Jane?' she asked unsteadily, her eyes wavering in hurt. Tempted as she was to snatch back her hand, she didn't, not wanting to show her doubts about him…or about Jane. She would listen to him first…she would hear this explanation he was so keen to give her. And then she would decide how to react.

Tom shook his head, a faint smile touching his lips. 'I simply asked her for some time alone with you…and she was happy to oblige.'

Natasha sucked in her breath. It must have been quite a conversation he'd had with Jane on his mobile phone! They had to be close friends for him to ask such a favour of her, after she'd invited him to her home for lunch. Or had he invited himself?

More mystified than ever, she raised wary eyes to his. 'Well, we're here now, all alone. Fire away.'

'Right.' Tom's chest heaved and fell. A muscle twitched at his temple. 'It's time I told you, Tash, why I really left you.'

CHAPTER TWELVE

HER heart stopped, the colour draining from her cheeks.

'You mean…there *was* another woman?' Something wrenched, deep inside her. If he'd lied to her…

'No!' Tom looked horrified. 'I told you there wasn't, Tash. There never has been anyone else…not since the day I met you.'

She flicked her tongue over her lips as relief washed through her. Partial relief. 'Well…why did you really leave me then?' She tried for a bantering note, but the words came out as barely more than a croak.

There was no answering glimmer as his eyes sought hers. 'Two things happened. First, I lost virtually all the money I'd been saving for years. That I'd been saving for *us*, Tash—for a home and a property of our own. I'd invested it in some speculative shares on the advice of a friend. They were going to make us a quick fortune, but…they collapsed. It was a disaster.' A self-deprecating twist curled his lips. 'A fool and his money are soon parted, so they say.'

Tash,' Tom assured her, scanning her face and reading her mind—as he always seemed able to do. 'We're getting married as soon as we can arrange it. We'll get married here, if you like. I'll fly all your family and friends in, and we'll have a slap-up party.'

'Oh, Tom, that sounds—'

He silenced her with a kiss—a deep, breath-stopping kiss that sent her thoughts scattering, her senses reeling.

She moaned in protest as Tom raised his head. 'I can hear the ute,' he said with a sigh. 'But there'll be plenty of time later, my love, when we're back at Kakadu...just the two of us, in your little tent, perhaps...or out under the stars...with all the time in the world and without any fear of interruption...wild animals, perhaps, excepted.' His voice had thickened, sending tremors of delicious anticipation through her.

He kissed her again as voices and laughter sounded outside. 'I just brought you here today to show you our future home, my darling,' he murmured, 'and to find out if you could face living here...at least for part of the time.'

'Only part of the time?' She looked up at him uncertainly. 'You mean, you won't want to live here all the time, Tom, and run the property yourself? You're going to let Jane and Bill go on managing it for you?'

'The property's big enough to need all four of us, Tash...but you and I won't always be here. You'll want to go back to Brisbane from time to time—to your gallery, and to see Charlie—and I'll need to check up on my safari business in Darwin. Luckily, I have a good man in the office up there and reliable staff to run it on a daily basis. And we'll want to go on painting trips together...take holidays together...go to art exhibitions...your own in particular.'

She gazed up at him, starry-eyed with her love for him. 'Tom, that all sounds simply marvellous, but my painting will never be as important to me as you are. And any children we might have.' Emotion caught in her voice. 'You do want children?' she asked tentatively, her eyes flickering in swift concern. 'They won't be...too much for you? I'd rather not have children if—'

'Now don't you start treating me with kid gloves, Tash,' Tom said roughly. 'I'm back to normal again, remember, and I intend to stay that way. I'm fit enough to have a whole tribe of kids if you want them. And when we do, we'll spend more time at home. But we're wasting time talking,' he murmured, nuzzling the silken warmth of her throat. 'Let's make the most of the few minutes we have left.'

They made the most of every single second,

Natasha turned to face him, her eyes flashing indignation. 'So it was your *pride* that made you break off our engagement. Because you'd lost your savings. Oh, Tom, you think that money and possessions mean so much to me?'

Tom shook his head, his eyes bleak. 'It was more than just losing the money. I had a routine medical checkup around the same time, as all pilots are obliged to have from time to time. It revealed that I was a diabetic.'

'Oh.' She felt a rush of sympathy for him, then bit her lip, frowning in confusion, and a blistering hurt. 'Being a diabetic's not the end of the world, Tom. Did you think I wouldn't support you? Was that why you didn't tell me? Why you left me? Because you thought I'd turn away from you?'

'No!' His eyes were pained. 'That's just it—I knew you *would* support me, Tash…that you would *never* turn your back on me. I didn't want to be a burden on you.'

'A *burden?*' She stared at him, shaking her head. 'You don't look like a burden to me, Tom Scanlon. You look as strong and healthy as an ox. You look fitter and healthier than I've ever seen you.'

'Well, I am…*now*, thank heaven. I've worked at it. I've changed my diet…ditched my bad habits…the old sloppy lifestyle. My sugar levels are back to normal—there's no sign of diabetes now. I can lead a normal life…expect a normal life span.'

The corner of his mouth twitched. 'As long as I keep on being sensible—which I intend to do.'

'Tom, that's wonderful.' She gulped in a quick breath. 'So...once you realised you weren't going to be a burden on me after all, you came back...is that it?' Her voice wobbled. 'I'm sorry you thought so little of me, Tom.'

He gripped her hand. 'I thought *too much* of you, that was the trouble! I knew you'd stand by me, no matter what happened. If I'd become an invalid, unable to care for myself...if I'd gone blind...no matter how sick or incapacitated I became, you'd have insisted on looking after me.'

There was a strange mistiness in his eyes as he looked down at her. 'You would have refused to leave me to go off on painting trips, or to go interstate to art exhibitions, or even to shut yourself away to paint. Your art would have suffered, your income would have dropped, and I had nothing to offer you then, Tash...and no hope, I thought eighteen months ago, of making a decent income in the future. I didn't even think I *had* a future.'

'Oh, Tom, whatever gave you such a pessimistic outlook?' She lifted his hand and pressed it to her lips. 'Surely not your doctors?'

'No,' he admitted. 'I'm afraid I overreacted when they gave me the test results. I had an uncle with diabetes, you see, who went blind and lost a leg. He was on dialysis for years after his kidneys wrapped in each other's arms, their lips clinging as if they would never let go.

It was only when Jane and Bill walked in with Jacko that Natasha remembered that she'd forgotten to call her father.

Charlie, she knew, would understand.

MILLS & BOON®

Makes any time special

Copyright © Harlequin Enterprises Limited 1997
All rights reserved

Enjoy a romantic novel from Mills & Boon®

Presents...™   *Enchanted™*   TEMPTATION.

Historical Romance™   ◣MEDICAL ROMANCE™

MAT1

packed up, and my aunt had a wretched life taking care of him. I immediately thought I'd end up like him, and you'd end up like my aunt, with no life of your own, just a life of drudgery.'

He shook his head. 'I refused to believe it at first, and insisted on a second opinion. That's why I flew down to Sydney—I wanted to be well away from home, from *you*, if the news was bad. When the doctors there confirmed the diagnosis, I panicked and broke off our engagement. I thought I'd never work again, never be able to fly again, that I'd end up a helpless invalid, and I wanted to spare you the kind of life my aunt had.'

Natasha smiled gently. He *was* working again, he was anything but a helpless invalid, and he was even planning to buy a light plane, presumably to fly himself. He was the fittest, strongest, healthiest man she'd ever seen. And the sexiest.

'They assured me I was only a borderline case and that I could control the disease with diet and exercise, but I wasn't convinced.' Tom heaved a sigh. 'I thought it was the beginning of the end. I'm afraid I was at rock bottom at the time...I wasn't thinking straight.'

'You certainly weren't,' she agreed fervently, wishing she'd been there to *put* him straight. 'So...how did you crawl out of this trough of despair?'

'It was the memory of *you*, Tash...of your

hurt…your understanding…the selfless way you of-fered me the freedom I pretended to want. But above all, it was the devastation in your voice when I blurted out that I'd met someone else. I'd wanted to cut the tie between us, you see…to set you free, once and for all. For *your* sake, Tash. I thought if you hated me enough you'd forget me and get on with your life…but I ended up hating myself even more, for what I'd done to you.'

He flicked a fly from her face before going on. 'I realised how cruel I'd been, how self-pitying I'd been. My uncle never changed his bad habits—he neglected his diet for years and never exercised. He didn't wake up to himself until it was too late. But I had a chance to control the disease by doing the right things from the start. That was when I decided to pull myself together and *do* something.'

She raised blurred eyes to his. He might have fallen into a trough of despair, but *she* was the one he'd been thinking of when he'd broken off their engagement.

'Oh, Tom…' For the first time she thought of the pain and fear that *he'd* suffered during that awful time. He'd suffered just as much as she had—if not more. 'What *did* you do exactly?' she asked curi-ously, wanting to know everything about those missing months.

Her heart felt light again. For the first time she noticed the brightness of the sky and the heady

MILLS & BOON®

Enchanted™

Fresh, tender love stories featuring strong, sensitive men and spirited women bringing you pure romance.

Four brand new titles each month from our bestselling authors.

Available at most branches of WH Smith, Tesco, Martins, Borders, Easons, Volume One/James Thin and most good paperback bookshops

GEN/02/RTL

MILLS & BOON®

Enchanted™

THE BABY SURPRISE by Janelle Denison

Grace had thought she couldn't have children. But now, after just one night with Ford McCabe, she was pregnant! Ford had always wanted Grace, and he wasn't going to wait any longer to make her his wife—even if that meant pretending for a while that it was just for the baby's sake…

HER SECRET BODYGUARD by Day Leclaire

Sami wanted a baby, but not a husband! So when gorgeous Noah Hawke arrived on her doorstep, she thought she'd found the ideal man—except Noah wasn't there for baby-making duties: he'd been hired to watch over Sami! And Noah believed the best way to protect her was to marry her…

MATILDA'S WEDDING by Betty Neels

Matilda has tried to ignore her strong attraction to Dr. Henry Lovell. After all, he is her boss *and* engaged to someone—else! But soon Henry starts to find Matilda just as intriguing as she finds him…

THE SHEIKH'S BRIDE by Sophie Weston

Leonora is an heiress in disguise, desperate to be loved for herself. Yet she can't resist being wooed by Amer el-Barbary under a velvet Nile sky… But Amer has a secret of his own. How will Leonora react when he reveals that he is a true prince of the desert, and wants to claim her as his bride?

Available from 7th April 2000

Available at most branches of WH Smith, Tesco, Martins, Borders, Easons, Volume One/James Thin and most good paperback bookshops

0003/02

scent of the roses. The birds singing in the trees echoed the singing in her heart. He'd left her because he *loved* her, not because he'd been afraid of marriage...or because he'd found another woman. He didn't have to tell her, in so many words, that he loved her...that he'd never stopped loving her. She *knew*.

'I booked myself into a health farm.' He grimaced. 'It was sheer torture—I hated it.' He reached up to touch her cheek. 'It was only the thought of you, my darling, that kept me going.'

My darling...

'Oh, Tom...' She felt a stir of guilt that she'd been so hard on him since he'd been back. If only she'd known the truth!

His eyes held a burning tenderness as they met hers, the flickering sunlight adding new brilliance to the deep blue.

'It was torture, but it was good for me. I learned what I had to do to lose weight and get fit again, and I did everything I had to do—rigorously. Afterwards I found work—active outdoor work that paid well but wasn't too taxing to begin with. I stuck to my diet—and saved madly. I earned enough to buy a four-wheel-drive and start up a safari business up north.'

He brushed his hand down her cheek in a shivery trail to her throat. 'I was keen to do something more demanding—more of a challenge—and see if I could stand up to it. And hopefully make a success of it at the same time.'

'So that's what you meant by proving something to yourself,' Natasha murmured, trembling under his touch. He'd wanted to prove that he was capable of leading a normal life...*his* kind of life—the tough outback life. 'I can see that you did stand up to it—brilliantly well.' Her gaze skimmed over his taut muscles, his flat stomach, his healthily bronzed skin. 'And you've obviously made a success of your safari business too, Tom.'

From what he'd let slip one night over dinner, Wild-Goose-Chase Tours was a very successful business indeed, with a fleet of four-wheel-drives and several tour operators working for him.

Not that it mattered to her if Tom was rich or poor, but she knew that restoring the money he'd lost eighteen months ago—the money he'd been saving for *their* future—would matter to him.

'Yes...the business has done well.' He pulled her into his arms, gathering her into the warmth of his shoulder. 'And *I've* done well, health-wise. Eighteen months after my world collapsed I was so fit and healthy again, with the all-clear from my doctors, even to fly light planes again if I wanted to, that I felt confident enough to come back into your life, Tash...and try to win you back.'

Happiness pumped through her. He'd come back for her...thank heaven. She gave him a golden smile, but it wavered. 'If you'd only told me all this when you first came back, Tom, I wouldn't have been so nasty to you.' Her brow furrowed. 'Why *didn't* you tell me?'

His lips brushed hers, promising endless delights ahead. 'I didn't want you coming back to me because you felt sorry for me, Tash, or because you felt it would be the right thing to do.' Emotion glowed in his eyes. ' I wanted to know that you still wanted me, cared for me, the way you did before...and if you could love me enough to give me another chance, despite the hell I put you through.'

A shadow crossed his face. 'I never should have lied to you, Tash, about meeting someone else...no matter how high-minded the reason. If you'd told me the same thing, I know how *I* would have felt.'

She felt his body shudder against her.

'Tom, I understand,' she said huskily. 'It's behind us now.'

He crushed her fiercely to him, almost squeezing the breath from her lungs. 'I can't live without you, Tash. Tell me you want me as much as I want you,' he begged. 'Tell me you still love me. Tell me you'll take me back. I've been going crazy!'

'Mm...me too,' she breathed, leaning into him. 'And the answer's yes...I do...I will...I love you, Tom.' She kissed the warm hollow at the base of his throat, where a pulse was beating wildly.

It was going to be all right, she thought dreamily.

Incredibly, wonderfully, it was going to be all right. They were back to where they'd been eighteen months ago, before he'd turned his back on her. Two people deeply in love…two hearts beating to the same drum…soul mates, as she'd once believed they were and could now believe again.

She knew she would have made the same sacrifice for Tom, if their roles had been reversed. If she'd been the one diagnosed with a potentially serious disease, only days after they'd become engaged, she would probably have lied to Tom and tried to release him in much the same way, not wanting to be a burden to *him.*

But she knew, in the depths of her heart, that Tom would still have wanted her and loved her regardless. He would have willingly supported and cared for her—just as she would do for him if it ever became necessary. That was what two people in love did…they cared for each other and wanted to be together forever…*in sickness and in health…for richer, for poorer.*

'I never stopped loving you, Tom,' she whispered. 'Even when I hated you.' A momentary glint lit her eyes. 'Don't you ever keep anything from me again! We share everything from now on, Tom Scanlon…the good and the bad. Understood?'

'Understood.' He pressed loving lips to hers, as if sealing the pact with a kiss. Then he hissed in his breath. 'Um…there is one more thing…'

Her heart jolted. Suddenly she felt vulnerable…unsure of him…unsure of his real motive in coming back. He'd tasted freedom these past eighteen months. Perhaps marriage wasn't on his agenda any more. Perhaps he just wanted to be close friends again…or just occasional lovers, on his periodic trips back to Brisbane. Was that what he meant by *one more thing?*

'Don't look at me like that,' Tom groaned, catching both her hands in his and gripping them tightly. 'The good and the bad, you just said. This is the good, Tash. Or I hope it is.'

Mystified, she gazed up at him. He kissed away the furrow between her brows, then gently kissed her eyelids, then the tip of her nose, and then her lips—his mouth lingering on her lips.

Finally he drew back, drinking in her face with fiercely smouldering eyes. 'If you knew how much I love you, Tash…how much I've longed for you, day after day, night after endless night. It seems a miracle that we're back together…that we have a future together after all. We do have a future, Tash…don't we?'

Now he was the one who sounded uncertain, and vulnerable.

'You will marry me, Tash?' he pressed, his voice hoarse with emotion.

Marry! Her head lifted. Was this—his proposal of marriage—the 'good' thing he'd mentioned?

Eyes shining, she curled her arms round his neck and clung to him. How could she ever have had any doubts? He loved her, and he wanted to marry her. He wanted a future with her. The same future she wanted.

'It's what I want with all my heart,' she assured him hoarsely.

'And this Warren character? He means nothing to you?'

She laughed. 'Nothing at all. He was a comfort to me when I needed comfort, that was all. I felt I knew where I was with him. That seemed important after—after you left me.'

Tom's jaw tightened. She reached up to stroke its tanned roughness with soothing fingers. 'I stopped going out with Warren the moment I realised I could never love him. There was no spark. We had nothing in common. And his kisses left me cold,' she admitted with an impish smile.

Tom's fingers tightened on her arms, his eyes burning into hers with a savage intensity. 'I'll never leave you again, Tash, I promise. No matter what happens. You're mine, and I...' He drew in his breath. '*Am* I yours, my love? Will you take me back...and keep me forever?'

She nodded, her eyes misting. 'For ever and ever.'

'Then say you'll marry me.'

A smile lit her face. 'I'll marry you. With all my heart.'

'I notice you haven't asked about the 'good' thing I mentioned a moment ago. Don't you want to know what it is?'

There was something *else*? She looked up at him with glistening eyes. What could be better than what they had already? But maybe it was some more good news about Tom's medical condition. It would be important to *him*. And to her too, if it set Tom's mind at ease. Scientists were finding new cures and treatments all the time. Perhaps he'd heard of some new miracle drug that he could take if his diabetes came back.

'I want to know everything about you, my foolish darling,' she assured him softly.

His eyes glittered under her loving gaze. 'Then come with me...' He tugged her to her feet, and with her hand firmly clasped in his, led her towards the house, the sweet fragrance of roses and frangipani wafting after them.

Just as they reached the steps, Jane ran up from behind.

'I must have left the keys to the ute in the house,' she panted. 'Bill wants me to pick him up at Gumtree Flats, where he's been fencing. He's going to join us for lunch.'

'Oh, good.' Tom stood back to let Jane dash inside, through the unlocked front door. 'Bill is Jane's husband,' he explained to Natasha, who flushed, feeling a quiver of shame that she'd ever imagined that Jane might have been anything more than a good friend to Tom.

To make it up to Jane, she smiled warmly as the girl reappeared with the keys in her hand, 'You have a lovely place here, Jane,' she enthused. 'You and Bill must be very happy here.'

Jane giggled. 'Oh, we don't live here. We live in the manager's house...over yonder.' She waved a hand. 'The *owner* lives here at the main homestead...when he's at home.'

'He's not home at the moment?' Natasha asked, suddenly feeling as if she were trespassing. Didn't the owner mind strangers wandering around his house and garden while he was away?

'He is at home, actually,' said Tom, and she heard another muffled giggle from Jane's direction. 'Why don't you step inside, Kate, and you can meet him.'

As Jane ran off, Tom ushered Kate into the front hall. Nobody came to meet them. There wasn't a sound in the house. She looked up at him with a faint frown.

'Are you sure he's at home?' she whispered. 'Where is he?'

A lopsided grin creased Tom's face. 'You're looking at him,' he said coolly.

Natasha gaped at him. 'You? *You* own this

place?' She felt suddenly giddy. Giddy with shock. 'Tom, that's amazing…it's wonderful…but—but why didn't you tell me you'd bought a property? Why keep it a secret until now?'

'I wanted to surprise you.' He shrugged, his lip quirking. 'No…there was more to it than that. I didn't want you to think I was trying to buy you back.'

She shook her head at him, a loving smile on her lips. 'You have some silly ideas sometimes, Tom Scanlon. But…how did it happen?' she faltered. She had visions of being in debt for the next hundred years. 'If you're buying a—a plane, Tom…and keeping your safari business…'

'Why don't you take a look around first, Tash, and then I'll explain all.' There was a shimmer of apprehension in his eyes now. 'I want to know what you think of your new home.'

'My new home?' It sounded too good to be true.

'Our new home,' he corrected softly. 'I just hope you like it, Tash.'

Even if she hadn't, she would have *made* herself like it, knowing how much it meant to Tom. But she did like it. Everything she'd already seen, and everything she saw as she explored the rambling, comfortably roomy house, she loved as much as he did. There was even a large room with plenty of light that would make a perfect studio.

'Of course, you'll want to give the place your

own personal touches,' Tom said, following her anxiously. 'It badly needs a woman's touch. And new furnishings. It was owned by an overseas business magnate, who seldom visited the place. When he died, the property was put up for sale, lock, stock and barrel.'

'And you bought it, Tom,' she whispered in awe. 'Your outback safari business must be a positive gold mine!'

He laughed. 'Not quite. But a gold mine did land in my lap,' he admitted, sobering. 'You remember I told you that my father had sold his confectionery business before he died?'

She nodded, her eyes slowly widening. 'Your father left you some money, Tom? He had a change of heart about cutting you out of his will?'

'He left me everything.' Tom's blue eyes held a misty sheen. 'Everything but his home in Newcastle and an apartment on Sydney Harbour, which he left to my stepmother—who promptly sold both and bought a luxury apartment on the Gold Coast. Meryl, amazingly, actually supported my father's decision to reinstate me.' A wry smile curved his lips. 'She must have been afraid I'd come back one day and tell Dad about the time she made a pass at me.'

'She made a *pass* at you?' Natasha blinked. 'Oh, Tom, no wonder you cut your ties with your family! With a stepmother making advances at you, and a father demanding you join his business or get out of his life…' She pursed her lips. 'Your stepmother didn't contest your father's will—after he'd died and couldn't learn the truth about…what she did to you?'

Tom gave a snort. 'She wouldn't have dared. I might have told the court what an immoral bitch she is, and Meryl would do anything to avoid bad publicity—she's a terrible snob. Not that she'd have bothered to contest the will anyway. She was already a wealthy woman—her previous husband left her a fortune.'

'Well, never mind her.' Natasha shrugged his stepmother aside. 'I'm so glad your father had a change of heart, Tom. He never tried to contact you…even after selling his business and changing his will in your favour? He never attempted to patch up your quarrel?'

Tom shook his head. 'Stubborn to the last. But by leaving me his money, I guess he was letting me know he still cared about me—in his own fashion— and that he was finally bowing to my decision to do my own thing. Maybe, if he hadn't died so suddenly, we would have patched things up eventually.'

'I'm sure you would have, Tom. And he would have been so proud of you.' She took his face in her hands. 'Your father's stubborn pride might have kept him from reconciling with you face to face, but at least you know that he'd reconciled with you in his heart…that he still loved you and wanted to support what you were doing with your life.'

She kissed him on the lips, a quick, fervent kiss, wanting to show him that he'd never be without love and support from her.

Tom's eyes softened under her tender gaze. 'I wish my father could have met you, Tash,' he said gently, tenderly brushing some loose strands of golden hair from her eyes.

'I wish I could have met him too…so I could have told him what a wonderful son he had.'

'Talking of fathers…' Tom's head lifted. 'Why don't you give Charlie a call, Tash, and tell him we're getting married—just as soon as we can arrange it?' He waved to a phone on the wall. 'He must be dying of suspense.'

Charlie…dear, conniving Charlie. Her eyes sparked—more in amusement now than annoyance at her father's well-meant subterfuge. She smiled, forgiving him. Forgiving them both. Their plotting had given her time alone with Tom and a chance for them to resolve their differences…and find love again.

'I will,' she whispered. 'In a minute.' She wound her arms round Tom's neck. 'You say…you want to get married *soon*, Tom?' she queried huskily, hardly daring to believe it could be happening.

'Nothing's ever going to come between us again,

FREE

2 BOOKS
AND A SURPRISE GIFT!

We would like to take this opportunity to thank you for reading this Mills & Boon® book by offering you the chance to take TWO more specially selected titles from the Enchanted™ series absolutely FREE! We're also making this offer to introduce you to the benefits of the Reader Service™—

- ★ FREE home delivery
- ★ FREE monthly Newsletter
- ★ FREE gifts and competitions
- ★ Exclusive Reader Service discounts
- ★ Books available before they're in the shops

Accepting these FREE books and gift places you under no obligation to buy; you may cancel at any time, even after receiving your free shipment. Simply complete your details below and return the entire page to the address below. *You don't even need a stamp!*

YES! Please send me 2 free Enchanted books and a surprise gift. I understand that unless you hear from me, I will receive 4 superb new titles every month for just £2.40 each, postage and packing free. I am under no obligation to purchase any books and may cancel my subscription at any time. The free books and gift will be mine to keep in any case.

NOEC

Ms/Mrs/Miss/Mr ....Initials ....
BLOCK CAPITALS PLEASE

Surname ....

Address ....

....

....Postcode ....

Send this whole page to:
UK: FREEPOST CN81, Croydon, CR9 3WZ
EIRE: PO Box 4546, Kilcock, County Kildare (stamp required)

Offer valid in UK and Eire only and not available to current Reader Service subscribers to this series. We reserve the right to refuse an application and applicants must be aged 18 years or over. Only one application per household. Terms and prices subject to change without notice. Offer expires 30th September 2000. As a result of this application, you may receive further offers from Harlequin Mills & Boon Limited and other carefully selected companies. If you would prefer not to share in this opportunity please write to The Data Manager at the address above.

Mills & Boon® is a registered trademark owned by Harlequin Mills & Boon Limited.
Enchanted™ is being used as a trademark.

MILLS & BOON®

Makes Mother's Day special

For Mother's Day this year, why not spoil yourself with a gift from Mills & Boon®.

Enjoy three romance novels by three of your favourite authors and a FREE silver effect picture frame for only £6.99.

Pack includes:

Presents...™
One Night With His Wife by Lynne Graham

Enchanted™
The Faithful Bride by Rebecca Winters

TEMPTATION®
Everything About Him by Rita Clay Estrada

0002/91/MB1

Available from 18th February